Eric's *Kasey radar* bleeped. Why was he so aware of a woman who wanted nothing to do with him? He should be grateful. He hadn't come home to start a relationship.

Unable to keep from looking at Kasey, he resigned himself to her reaction. Had four years in Africa really made such a difference that he'd gone from fighting off women to chasing after one who denied wanting anything more to do with him?

He caught her looking at him. Her big green eyes were soulful beneath her glasses and her fingers tightly clutched her stethoscope.

Why was she pretending their chemistry didn't exist when it so obviously did?

He wanted Dr Kasey Carmichael. More than he remembered ever wanting a woman.

With time, she'd admit she wanted him too.

Janice Lynn has a Masters in Nursing from Vanderbilt University, and works as a nurse practitioner in a family practice. She lives in the southern United States with her husband, their four children, their Jack Russell—appropriately named Trouble—and a lot of unnamed dust bunnies that have moved in since she started her writing career. To find out more about Janice and her writing, visit www.janicelynn.com

Recent titles by the same author:

SURGEON BOSS, SURPRISE DAD
THE DOCTOR'S MEANT-TO-BE MARRIAGE
THE HEART SURGEON'S SECRET SON
THE DOCTOR'S PREGNANCY BOMBSHELL

THE PLAYBOY DOCTOR CLAIMS HIS BRIDE

BY

JANICE LYNN

MILLS & BOON®

Pure reading pleasure™

First published in Great Britain 2009
Harlequin Mills & Boon Limited,
Eton House, 18-24 Paradise Road, Richmond, Surrey TW9 1SR

ISBN: 978 0 263 20931 0

Set in Times Roman 10½ on 12¼ pt
15-0609-42667

Printed and bound in Great Britain
by CPI Antony Rowe, Chippenham, Wiltshire

THE PLAYBOY DOCTOR CLAIMS HIS BRIDE

To my grandparents, Floyd & Janie Green

CHAPTER ONE

DR. KASEY CARMICHAEL typed clinical data into the medical record on the hypertensive patient she'd just seen. When finished, she sent his prescriptions electronically to the in-house pharmacy of the Rivendell Medical Center.

Knocking on the open door, Dr. Jonathan Douglas stuck his blond head into the exam room. The pretty-boy doctor flashed baby blues and a row of pearly white teeth that had women swooning all over northern Kentucky. "You got a minute?"

Kasey shot a coolly professional smile at the physician she'd worked with for two years.

"I'll be right there." She hit "Save" and closed her patient's file. Standing, she smoothed the crisp lines of the unbuttoned white lab coat she wore over her navy slacks and linen blouse.

She loved her job in the ambulatory clinic of the large multispecialty Rivendell Medical Center. Loved that it provided the opportunity to give back to the community, to help others the way she'd once been helped.

Rivendell's sheer size gave her the opportunity to

achieve the professional and personal success she craved. Success that dangled within her reach.

When Dr. Herbert stepped down from the board, Kasey was a shoo-in to replace him. Everyone said so.

Smiling, she stepped into the clinic's hallway to see what Dr. Douglas was up to this time. Although an excellent doctor, he'd never held any appeal. Probably due to his tomcat ways reminding her of the men who'd constantly come in and out of her childhood in the form of her mother's latest loser.

"What can I do for you, Dr. Doug—?" Her voice stalled, stuck in her rapidly tightening throat. Her gaze froze on the man standing with her colleague.

The room spun.

Please let her be hallucinating.

"Eric?" Her one-and-only-ever one-night stand stared at her with similar shock. Her pulse hit a rapid, brain-frying boil. "What—? How—? Why are you here?" she sputtered.

"Hello, Kasey." Quickly recovering from his surprise at seeing her, his dark eyes glistened as if he'd stumbled upon the pot of gold at the end of the rainbow. A huge smile split his handsome face.

A smile that stole Kasey's ability to breathe just as it had on the night they'd met.

She took a step back, placed her hand on the door frame to steady her wobbly, turned-to-water legs.

"What are you doing here?" she asked again, feeling hazy.

"Funny, I was just going to ask you the same thing," Eric answered in that smooth-as-silk voice that had whispered sweet praise to her two months ago. Recalling what else they'd done, Kasey struggled to remain on her feet. Her body threatened to slide to the floor in a gooey, deoxygenated pile of shocked, blue mush.

"You two know each other?" Dr. Douglas took a step back, his gaze flicking from Kasey to Eric.

"We've met." Eric's eyes narrowed as he regarded her, a mixture of suspicion and pleasure in his eyes.

"I've never heard either of you mention the other," Dr. Douglas mused. For all his playboy ways, no one could accuse him of being slow on the uptake. No doubt her colleague had already worked out just how well she and Eric had known each other.

Probably because even though her brain was in embarrassed denial of Eric being here, her libido was dancing a happy jig of remembered pleasure.

Kasey wished the tiled floor would open up and swallow her. Anything to escape Eric's predatory male look. Anything to escape Dr. Douglas's knowing curiosity.

If word got out she'd had a one-night stand, the news would hurt her chances of being asked to join the clinic's medical board. The older board members would look unfavorably on a potential member behaving in such a feckless manner. Even if her lapse of judgment had been on the night of her mother's funeral.

Hadn't she learned how quickly one could lose everything they held dear following the gigantic mistake she'd made with Randall Covington III? Oh, yeah, she'd paid dearly for that error in judgment.

Now her only one-night stand stood in her workplace.

Panic clutched at her throat, rendering her speechless.

This wasn't really happening. History would not repeat itself. Not that she'd had a one-night stand with Randall. No, she'd given the bastard an entire year of her life. A whole wasted year where she'd dreamed of them being the perfect couple, having the perfect life together. Boy, had she been wrong.

About them being a perfect couple at any rate. With or without a man in her life, she was going to have the perfect life. She'd set goals and worked long hours to make sure they came true.

"When did you meet?" Delight sparkled in Dr. Douglas's blue eyes.

"A few months ago." Eric's gaze bored into Kasey. Was he waiting for her to acknowledge the night they'd spent together? Did he really think she'd do that? Lord, she just wanted to forget that night had ever happened. Had spent two months trying to forget.

Unfortunately, forgetting the best sex she'd ever had wasn't proving an easy task.

Images of that best sex flashed into her head like candid shots portraying the man standing before her in living color.

Hot, lurid, take-her-to-another-world best sex images.

Fire engulfed her face. She lifted her hand to fan the burn, realized what she was doing, and stopped.

"You met Eric and didn't tell me?" Jonathan's dark blond brow arched.

This wasn't happening.

Kasey roped her uncooperative vocal cords into submission. "Why would I mention we'd met? He was just someone I met—" *mere hours after laying my estranged mother in the ground* "—and I didn't know the two of you knew each other." *Because he and I really didn't do a lot of in-depth talking.*

Eric's smile slipped. "Why indeed?"

She tried not to look at him, but an inner force compelled her. His chocolate eyes appeared thoughtful, as if he was trying to read her, to gauge how to take her response.

What would her sexy lover have said, done, had she still been in his bed when he'd awakened?

Hello, she'd been a one-night stand. No doubt he was grateful she hadn't made a scene, that she had slipped out in abject humiliation prior to him waking that morning.

She was humiliated. She'd been the one thing she'd always sworn never to be. Easy. Like her mother.

She'd had one night of passion.

With a stranger.

A stranger she'd met in a bar and later accompanied to his hotel. A stranger who now stood in her clinic making a sham of her memories by looking so much better than she'd recalled.

Much to her abhorrence, she recalled way too much all too often.

God, he was gorgeous.

The strong, handsome planes of his face had surely been sculpted by a goddess intent on tempting mortal women with a glimpse of heaven. The sun had kissed his dark wavy hair with gold and his skin with a bronze hue.

At six-two or -three, he towered over her five-eight. Beneath his tailored suit, his shoulders stretched broadly, tapering into a trim waist and powerful, narrow hips. As he'd been the night they met, he was so well dressed that if testosterone didn't ooze from every pore of his fine body she'd think he must be gay. But in vivid and exquisite detail, she knew testosterone oozed.

An image of his naked body over hers, melted into hers, popped into her mind, short-circuiting her nerve endings.

Kasey swallowed. Just as she'd done many times over the past two months, she forced memories of him from her mind.

Only how was she supposed to force him from her mind when he stood a few feet away, eyeing her as if he'd like to push her into the exam room she'd just stepped out of and pick up where they'd left off? Naked and tangled together with frantic desire. When her body was all too willing.

No. She didn't want him at her workplace.

Didn't want him anywhere near her.

She had a great life.

One that didn't need a complication of his magnitude. No pun intended.

"This is interesting." As the silence continued, a grin lifted the corner of Dr. Douglas's mouth. "I call out my esteemed coworker to introduce her to my old university roomie, and they've already met."

"Dr. Douglas is who you were supposed to meet that night?" Kasey asked, winced and slapped her hand over her mouth in the most giveaway oops motion a person could make.

Eric nodded, then turned to his *old university roomie.* "I met Kasey on the night you got hung up here at the clinic. We shared a few drinks, a few dances."

A zillion amazing orgasms.

Heat slammed into Kasey's body.

"Right," she agreed on a breathless note, averting her gaze to stare at a body mass index chart stuck on the wall. "A few drinks and dances. No big deal."

Eric had been a big deal.

A very big deal.

She winced. What was wrong with her? She was at work. She wasn't supposed to be having a hot flush of sexual awareness.

That wasn't who she was. She was calm, cool, collected Dr. Kasey Carmichael.

Dr. Douglas's bushy brows rose so high they brushed the stylishly tousled hair atop his head. "You were in a bar? Had drinks? As in alcohol rather than a wheat-germ shake?" A new light shone in his eyes as he looked at Kasey. Possibly for the first time ever he was seeing her as a woman rather than the uptight doctor he worked with. "And you danced? Did I miss something?" He drew his brows into a V. "Like hell freezing over?"

Squelching the urge to growl at him, Kasey took a deep, exasperated breath. She pushed her glasses up the bridge of her nose to give her hands something to do.

Otherwise she might curl her fingers into a fist and punch his straight nose. "I happen to like wheat-germ shakes and, of course, I dance."

Not well, but she could pull off the slow numbers she and Eric had swayed to without any problems. Usually too self-conscious to let herself relax, she'd moved in rhythm to Eric's lead. On the dance floor and in the bedroom. He'd been perfect. And something she'd desperately tried to stop thinking about because Kasey was not like her mother.

"In case you hadn't realized—" she kept her voice smooth, calm, professional, like she wasn't dying inside "—I am over the legal drinking age."

Dr. Douglas burst into laughter. "You've totally shattered my image of you, Kase. I didn't think you drank. Or hung out in bars. Or talked to men who weren't paying you for their fifteen-minute appointment slot of your time." He placed his hands over his heart. "Shattered, I tell you."

Her nerves grated at how he shortened her name. She glared.

Eric cleared his throat, calling their attention back to him.

Kasey turned to the man who'd held her so tenderly on the night she'd felt so alone. He looked perturbed.

Was he upset that he'd run into his weepy bedmate who'd practically ripped off his clothes? That his friend knew he'd had drinks with the office wallflower who preferred wheat-germ shakes to cosmos?

Lord, she wanted out of here.

A cool blast of realization froze the blood chugging through Kasey's veins.

Why was Dr. Douglas introducing her to his old university mate here at the medical clinic?

University mate.

"You're a doctor, aren't you?" She'd heard some benefactor's son had been visiting the clinic that morning. A doctor. She held her breath, waiting for Eric's answer.

The corner of his mouth lifted in an ironic twist. "I did mention my profession on the night we met."

Had he? She'd been so upset when she'd gone into the bar, upset and unable to face the realization that her mother, her last blood relative, had died.

Eric had been sitting on the bar stool next to the one she'd plopped down on. She hadn't noticed him or anyone except the flashing neon beer advertisement behind the bar. Apparently he'd noticed her, though. He'd been concerned and kept talking, trying to draw her into conversation. She couldn't recall much of what he'd said while they'd sat there.

All she'd been able to think about was that she'd buried Betsy Carmichael that afternoon. That the woman who'd given birth to her, made her childhood a living hell, had died. That she was alone in the world now that her only family was gone.

In reality she'd felt alone a long time before her mother had drawn her last breath.

"You're who the administrator has been with today, aren't you?" *Please say no. Please don't let him be the bigwig son of the clinic's benefactor.* "You're applying for a job here, aren't you?"

"Applying for a job?" Dr. Douglas burst out laughing. "As if. Eric can write his ticket at this place."

"That's enough," Dr. Eric Matthews interrupted his friend. He'd rather not have his family connection to Rivendell Medical Center pointed out to the woman he'd met two months ago. Had she known who he was? Used him in hopes of advancing her career at Rivendell?

He hadn't thought so but, hell, he'd been wrong about women before.

Still, he'd really believed Kasey was different. Certainly the fact that he'd awakened to an empty bed had been a new twist. Had she known why he'd returned to Kentucky? Like so many from his past, had she seen him as a ticket to easy street?

Her eyes held dark shadows. She'd been startled to see him. No more so than he'd been when he'd looked up to meet his best friend's "boring, career-driven ice queen" colleague.

Jonathan was a fool. Kasey was no ice queen. She was hot. His psyche had the scorch marks to prove it. His entire body caught fire just at being near her again, at memories of how their bodies had meshed together.

But Kasey wasn't happy to see him.

He honestly wasn't sure how he felt about seeing her. At least not at Rivendell Medical Center. Had he run into her in a social setting he'd have been thrilled, but the last thing he needed was an involvement with someone at the clinic.

He'd come home a different man than the one who'd left four years ago. He didn't engage in one-night stands or living for the moment. He'd changed. For the better. Or so he'd thought.

His first night back in Rivendell, Kasey had reduced him to habits he'd sworn were deeply buried in the past.

He wasn't a love-'em-and-leave-'em kind of guy anymore. Hadn't been for years. He sure wasn't going to be a loved-by-'em-and-left-by-'em kind of guy. Hell, no.

Dr. Kasey Carmichael had loved him and left him.

She didn't look the same as she had the night they'd met. Her shoulder-length brunette hair was pulled harshly away from her face. She wore trendy black-rimmed glasses. Her light makeup was impeccably dusted over her high cheekbones and wide green eyes, but not in a way to draw men to her. More of a shield against letting anyone see the real her. She looked like a woman downplaying her femininity to appear all business, to appear cold and unreachable.

But Eric had seen behind the mask. If she hadn't disappeared before he'd awakened, he'd have spent more time with her, gotten to know her. Why had she snuck out before dawn? He'd never had a woman leave him with no strings attached. Even the pickups from his youth had usually hinted at wanting money or jewelry or trips to fancy restaurants.

What did Kasey want?

"Tell me," she prompted. Desperation shone in her eyes, but her voice sounded coolly professional, as if she was used to hiding her emotions. "Tell me why you're here."

"I met with Clive and several members of the board on the day after we met. That's why I was in town that night."

She winced, causing the glasses to scoot up the bridge of her pert nose. "Because?"

His fingers itched to slip the heavy frames off her face. The glass didn't appear to be corrective, just distractive.

"They offered me a position at the clinic." An over-simplification, but the truth.

Kasey closed her eyes, looking like she wanted to disappear. Was she really so horrified that they'd come face-to-face again?

She visibly shuddered, then opened pain-filled eyes.

"You knew who I was, didn't you? You knew I worked here. This was all a big joke to you."

Fathoms of hurt welled in her eyes. He didn't understand the depth of pain. Why would she think he'd tricked her? She'd been the one to disappear without even a goodbye or thanks for a fun night. Besides, she was the one with everything to gain from sleeping with the son of the clinic's primary stockholder.

"Nothing between us was a joke. Not to me," he assured her, carefully choosing his words. "I didn't know you worked here, Kasey. How could I? You never told me you were a doctor."

A couple of nurses stood just out of line of sight, trying to busy themselves but allowing curiosity to get the better of them. Eric sighed. He'd come home to take on his responsibilities, to be near his mother, not to immediately immerse the clinic in gossip about his personal life.

"Is there somewhere we can talk in private?"

"No." Kasey shook her head, her eyes narrowed into accusatory slits. "I don't want to talk to you, in private or otherwise. You aren't supposed to be here." She enunciated each word with great emphasis. "I don't want you here."

Had she audibly hissed at him, he wouldn't have been surprised. What did surprise him was her reaction to seeing him. He was the one who should be feeling betrayed. She'd given him the best sex of his life, left without a trace, and then showed up as an employee at his family's medical center. Why was she so upset?

He racked his brains, trying to recall what he'd last

said to her during the night. Kissing the top of her head and whispering that she was amazing didn't seem like something that would make her so prickly. Saying how beautiful she was, how special, how glad he was that she'd sat beside him at the bar, nope, that shouldn't have agitated her, either.

Yes, she'd been upset about something on the night they'd met. And, yes, had he been a true gentleman he would have driven her home and gotten her phone number, not carried her to his hotel room and made love to her over and over. But, hell, he'd wanted her with an undeniable desperation and it had been a long time since he'd been with anyone. A long time since he'd wanted to be with anyone. Kissing Kasey, touching her, had felt right.

"What happened that night?" Jonathan asked, gawking at them, his lips twitching with laughter. "Sounds like more than drinks and dancing."

Kasey shot Jonathan a lethal look. "Don't you have a patient to see or something?"

"Right. I'll go see a patient." Jonathan nodded with a gleam in his eye that said he'd grill Eric for the low-down later.

"We should talk," Eric said, still trying to figure out why she was in attack mode. Sure, she'd left his bed without waking him, but she'd enjoyed the night, had been willing, more than willing. She'd been interesting, funny, sweet and sexy when they'd talked in the bar. Besides the phenomenal sex, he'd genuinely liked her. He'd planned to see her again, had been disappointed to wake, find her gone and realize he only knew her first name.

Having a woman use him hadn't been a new experience, but he'd never been used in that particular way before.

"This isn't the time or place for this conversation." Kasey took another step back, looked like she might take off, but didn't. Visibly, she pulled herself together, transforming before his eyes into a calm vision of cool professionalism. She stood with her shoulders high, regal. Only her expressive eyes betrayed the hint of inner turmoil.

"I have patients to see, too." Expression pinched, Kasey reached up and pulled the stethoscope off her neck, fingering the tubing. "It was unexpected to see you, Dr. Matthews."

She emphasized the word *doctor*, making it sound dirty, almost like an insult. Damn it, he had told her he was a doctor. He was more proud of his degree than anything else he'd done in his sorry life.

She turned, took a step away from him.

His breath caught. He didn't want her to walk away. "Have dinner with me."

She paused, then shook her head. "That wouldn't be a good idea."

"Why not?" He hadn't consciously made the decision to ask her to dinner, but now that he had, he wanted her to say yes. Besides, they needed to talk about what had happened two months ago.

She hesitated, momentarily looking uncertain. "You're coming to work at Rivendell, aren't you?"

Now that he knew she was here, neither hell nor high water would keep him from Rivendell. A factor that shouldn't have any influence at all, but suddenly did. "Yes."

She leveled him with the steely green gaze beneath her glasses. "That's why having dinner together isn't a good idea. Fraternizing with colleagues is not conducive to my career goals."

Battling a myriad of emotions, Eric watched her disappear into an exam room. At least this time he'd been awake when she left.

"Tell me everything." Jonathan pounced the moment the door closed behind Kasey. Where had he been hiding? Behind a plant?

"I thought you were seeing a patient," Eric pointed out, leading his friend toward Jonathan's private office. "Besides, we're in the hallway of the clinic where we work. Use some tact."

He closed Jonathan's office door. "I met Kasey two months ago, liked her and want to go out with her again."

"And?"

"There's nothing more to tell."

Not that he was willing to share. Not even with someone he'd shared secrets with for years and who knew him better than anyone. Jonathan knew his darkest moments and had seen him through them. But some things were private. His night with Kasey fell into that category.

His friend leaned against his desk, arms crossed, expression confused. "You really want to go out with the Ice Queen?"

"Don't call her that." Eric glared, feeling oddly defensive of the woman who'd elicited strong emotions from the moment she'd plopped down next to him looking as if her world had crashed. "Why wouldn't I want to go out with Kasey? She's a beautiful woman."

Jonathan looked flummoxed. "Yeah, but—"

"She's intelligent, witty, has a great sense of humor and is a lot of fun to be around," Eric interrupted before Jonathan could say anything else. What was wrong with his friend? He'd been working with Kasey for heaven only knew how long and yet he hadn't noticed what a sexy misnomer she was? That she hid her passion behind too-tight hairstyles, don't-touch-me designer clothes and I'm-smart-not-pretty glasses?

"Are we talking about the same woman?" Jonathan shook his head. "Don't get me wrong. Kasey's a great coworker—steady, dependable, thorough—but she's not your type. Too uptight and career oriented."

"Those aren't bad qualities you're describing," Eric pointed out.

"She has her sights set on the top, pal. She's made no secret that she wants a seat on the board and she's put in the long hours to make sure it happens," Jonathan warned, pretending to shiver. "Plus, she gives off those subzero vibes. Could give a man permanent frostbite."

Frostbite? Eric had come closer to suffering heatstroke in Kasey's company than frostbite. Jonathan and apparently every other man in Kasey's life were blind fools.

Just so long as she didn't plan to use him as her stepping stone to the top, Eric had no problem with a career-minded woman. Particularly when that woman attracted him the way Kasey did.

"She's all business, rarely smiles," Jonathan continued, listing all the reasons he thought Kasey was wrong for Eric.

She didn't smile? Why did that make his chest hurt? Why did it make him want to do everything in his power to make her smile, and often? Just as he'd done on the night they'd met.

"Your loss, bud, because I've seen her smile." She hadn't smiled at first. But before they'd left for his hotel she'd laughed out loud several times. "She has an amazing smile that makes a man automatically smile back."

He wanted to experience her smile again.

Jonathan's gaze narrowed, but a smile tugged at the corners of his mouth. "I think you're suffering from brain freeze. Either that or you worked in that African desert for so long you can't handle hot anymore."

Eric grinned. Oh, he could handle hot all right. And he planned to.

Just as soon as he could convince Kasey.

CHAPTER TWO

ERIC leaned back in the expensive leather chair meant to impress guests invited into Rivendell Medical Center's administrator's office. With its original wall prints, expensive furnishings and lush greenery, the office screamed success.

"I know Dr. Douglas has already shown you around the ambulatory clinic, but would you like a tour of the rest of the facility prior to officially starting?" the lanky man he'd spent the morning with offered. "I know you practically grew up at the center, but that was before we moved to the new location."

That had been three years ago while Eric had been in Africa as part of the medical mission team he'd joined straight out of medical school. A lifetime ago. Eric didn't even feel like the same person who'd once lived in Rivendell.

He wasn't the same person.

"The entire building is state-of-the-art. The in-house referral system streamlines care with great efficiency. We have close to a hundred providers of various specialties on staff now." Clive gave Eric a grin. "Your grandfather would be proud. I know your mother is."

His maternal grandfather would be proud of how far the clinic had come. The facility comprised a three-story building with multiple specialty departments, a fully equipped laboratory, radiology department, pharmacy and a same-day surgery wing that bore Eric's grandfather's name.

His mother was proud of the clinic, too, but Eric refused to let thoughts of her into his mind. He'd barely been home a week and already she was trotting Kentucky debutantes in front of him at every opportunity.

Eric shook his head at his mother's matchmaking and at the administrator. "Jonathan showed me around the center when I was here two months ago."

Just as it had then, the center felt right.

Like this was where he was meant to be despite years of adamant and rebellious denial of his heritage. Despite his mother thinking his move home meant he was ready to settle down and produce heirs.

"If there's anything Rivendell can do to make your move smoother, let me know," Clive went on, no doubt in an effort to impress Lena Woolworth's only child.

"Actually…" Eric rocked back in the chair, eyeing the administrator through narrowed eyes. "There is something."

Clive's temple jumped with a nervous spasm. "Oh?"

"I'm going to work in the ambulatory clinic."

The man's unease faded into confused relief.

"The ambulatory clinic? But…" Remembering who he was talking to, the administrator nodded. "Of course.

I should have realized you'd want to work directly with Dr. Douglas."

Perhaps he should feel guilty for using his influence to change where he'd be working at the last minute. Hadn't he sworn not to let moving home corrupt him? That he'd remain true to the man he'd grown into while thousands of miles away? But working in the ambulatory clinic appealed enough for him to ignore any doubts about his motives.

He had no doubts.

He wanted to be near Dr. Kasey Carmichael.

Whether or not wanting to be near her was a good thing remained to be seen.

Early that evening, Kasey finished seeing her afternoon patients and slouched into the comfy ergonomic chair at her desk.

Her office wasn't much larger than a broom closet, but she'd been allowed to decorate the room to her taste. She'd gone with crisp white walls and black furniture. A vase of colorful Shasta daisies, looking so real people often reached out to touch a petal just to see, sat on the top of her bookshelf along with a model of a human kidney and a two-foot-tall skeleton she'd nicknamed "Bones".

She kept a vanilla-scented air freshener plugged in to drown out the antiseptic smell that permeated the rest of the clinic.

The room wasn't fancy, but at least she had a small private place to call her own.

Right now, she desperately needed privacy.

Eric was here. At the clinic.

Maybe he'd work on a different floor and she'd never see him. What kind of doctor was he anyway?

Dropping her face into her palms, she massaged her temples.

This couldn't be happening.

Just seeing Eric in the hallway had made her want to push him into a room and perform a thorough examination of all his many attributes, right down to taste-testing him from head to toe.

Which shocked her.

She'd never been adventurous sexually. She and Randall had shared a good enough sex life, but they hadn't been the stuff to burn down buildings.

One night with Eric and smoke still clouded her mind.

Intoxicating smoke that made her want to inhale deeply and give in to sweet fantasy.

Sweet? There hadn't been anything sweet about her fantasies. Hot, enthusiastic, sweaty, yes, but not sweet.

Kasey's fingers dug deeper into her scalp.

No way would she risk her career because of a man a second time. Not at Rivendell, where she'd made her fresh start and the potential to achieve her lifelong dreams dangled in front of her like the proverbial carrot.

A knock sounded at her door and she looked up. Eric watched her.

Realizing she was massaging her temples in overtime, she dropped her hands to her desk and tapped the sleek black surface. Which was no less nervous appearing than her temple massaging. Taking a deep breath, she flattened her palms against the desk to stay their fidgety tapping.

"I thought you'd left." Brilliant conversation. Yet what did it matter? His family owned stock in the center. Could the situation be any more Randall-like? She needed to put Eric firmly in the past and keep him there.

If she remained steadfast, perhaps he'd take a hint and leave her alone.

Which was what he'd eventually do regardless. She was definitely like her mother in that regard. Men never stayed long. She'd thought Randall had been different. Steady, dependable Randall. But she'd been wrong. Horribly wrong and just look what that mistake had cost her in the long run.

Not to mention that she'd gone to Eric's hotel room on the night they'd met. She didn't respect herself, how could she expect him to?

"I did leave," Eric admitted. His gaze roved over her in melted chocolate temptation that made her libido growl in hungry response. "I came back."

"Why?" Why did he have to look so wonderful in his black slacks, blue shirt and tie? Like something on the cover of a men's magazine. He'd taken off his suit jacket at some point since she'd seen him earlier and his tie was loosened around his neck, making her want to walk over to him and straighten it.

Or perhaps she just wanted a reason to touch him?

"You."

"Me?" As much as she thrilled at his answer, he had to stop. She'd made a mistake the night they'd met. One she could forgive due to her mother's death. But she couldn't justify a repeat of their amazing night.

His family held power over the medical center.

They were going to be coworkers.

If she'd learned anything from her experience with Randall, she'd learned not to mix personal stuff with one's job.

The consequences were too dire.

"Seeing you today was an unexpected surprise." He stepped into her office, closed the door behind him, overwhelming the tiny room. Even Bones appeared to tremble in his presence. "I enjoyed our night together."

What rabbit hole had she fallen into? Because he looked as if he wanted to touch her. As if he'd like to push her against her desk, hike up her skirt and run his hands along her thighs, along her— Kasey gulped. "No!"

At his startled look, she took a calming breath.

"That night was…" Amazing, wonderful, just what she'd needed. *Embarrassing.* She didn't behave like her mother. Not usually. She wasn't a woman driven by lust and she had no intention of becoming one. She'd worked too hard to make something of herself, to rise above her past, poverty and genetics. "Nice, but we both know it was a one-night stand kind of thing."

"One-night stand kind of thing?"

He towered over her, not in a menacing way, but she fought the desire to lean as far away as possible…to ease the temptation of moving closer to those broad shoulders and talented hands.

"You're wrong," he continued, looking completely aware of her proximity dilemma and pleased by her reaction to him. "That night wasn't a one-night stand. Far from it."

"What would you call it?" *Besides the most humili-*

ating event of my life? No, that would have been when Skymont Hospital had let her go over her relationship with Randall. Or perhaps when her mother had shown up drunk at her high school graduation ceremony. Either way, her night with Eric had been a mistake. That's what she repeated in her head, not allowing her hormones a word in edgewise.

"The beginning of something worth pursuing." His eyes bored into her, daring her to deny his claim. Unbidden, her gaze dropped to the strong set of his jaw, to his lips. That mouth had kissed her. All of her.

"Stop." She closed her eyes, fighting memories of the tender kisses he'd placed on her hair, her face, the way he'd kissed away her tears. Memories of tenderness that had given way to passion. To urgent kisses. "Our meeting that night was nothing more than a bad coincidence. We should forget it happened."

"What you call a bad coincidence I call a stroke of good fortune. Just as I consider seeing you today good fortune."

His words were sweet to her ears, but what he was really saying was that he wanted sex again. They'd slept together on the day they'd met. He wasn't interested in a real relationship with her. Just sex. Toe-curling, life-altering sex but, still, just sex.

He moved further into the office, crowding her personal space by coming around to her side of the desk and half sitting, half leaning against the corner. His closeness zapped her ability to breathe.

"Why didn't you wake me before you left, Kasey?"

Oh, God, why had he moved so close?

She shut her eyes, counted to ten, prayed for indifference to him. "That night shouldn't have happened and wouldn't have under different circumstances."

Sad, but true.

"Yes, it would have."

Spicy, sexy musk toyed with her senses. She squeezed her eyes more tightly closed because she worried that if she looked at him, she'd have to touch. Absolutely have to.

"I'm sorry you got dragged into my bad day," she plunged on, needing to talk, needing to do anything that kept her from reaching out to run her finger over the cleft in his chin. "I regret the entire evening."

"You regret meeting me?" He sounded as if he didn't believe her.

Knowing they'd be coworkers, she should regret having met him, but her heart ached at the thought of not having the comfort she'd felt as she'd drifted to sleep in his arms. At not experiencing the mind-shattering passion his kisses had evoked. She'd had a bad day. He'd made her feel better. No matter how much she should, she didn't regret them making love.

She couldn't tell him that.

Doing so would only make what she had to do more difficult.

Indifference. She needed indifference.

"Yes," she choked out. "I regret meeting you."

"Open your eyes."

She forced her eyelids open, looked into his dark eyes and swallowed. Hard. Lord, he looked as if he really had been hurt that she'd left him.

"Now, say you regret meeting me and mean it." He shook his head when her lids automatically lowered. "Don't close your eyes, Kasey. Look at me, and tell me you regret what we shared, because I don't believe you."

She wanted to scoot her chair toward the wall to put more distance between them, but she needed to make a strong stand. Her job, her peace of mind was at stake. She should push him off her desk, but didn't dare touch him. To do so would send her few functioning brain cells into sexual dementia.

Focus on your goals, Kasey. She gave herself a mental pep talk. *Career, helping others, social status, being a valued member of society. A fling with a coworker robbed you of that once. Eric is a coworker with an influential family.*

"Is your ego so big you can't accept that I made a mistake in going to your hotel room?" she accused, going on the attack. She had to destroy the chemistry between them. Because she had to deny it. She couldn't go through what she'd gone through with Randall.

Somehow she suspected recovering from Eric would rob her of a lot more than Randall's decision she was good enough to sleep with but not good enough to give his last name to.

"No, my ego isn't that big." He leaned across her desk, staring straight into her eyes, his breath caressing her lips. "But I was there that night."

"I remember." She hadn't meant to sound nostalgic, but her voice held a touch of longing she couldn't deny. She shook off the erotic memories and put on the flat affect she'd perfected in the days following the fiasco with Randall. In the days before Skymont Hospital had let her go. "I took advantage of you that night."

"What?" His forehead wrinkled in surprise.

She sighed. How much could she tell him without also admitting how much being near him affected her? Was this what her mother had battled every time a sexy man had come near? This overwhelming need to touch? To be touched?

If so, Kasey was grateful the first thirty years of her life had passed without her knowing such carnal craving.

"Like I said," she began, wishing he weren't so close, that she didn't feel every inch Betsy Carmichael's daughter, right down to the burst of pheromones dictating she forget everything except how this man's lips had felt against hers. "I had a bad day."

"Which doesn't explain how you used me."

She shrugged as nonchalantly as she could pull off when she couldn't breathe. "Don't you get it? I didn't want to be alone. You were convenient. End of story."

A glimmer of anger shone in his eyes. "You're saying any man would have done?"

"If it meant not being alone that night?" She called upon all her strength and lied through her teeth. "Any man would have done."

He smoothly shifted to stand by the black leather chair wedged between her desk and the corner of the office. Genuine shock shone on his face. Would he realize she was oversimplifying the night's events? She couldn't give him that opportunity.

"When I saw you with Dr. Douglas this morning…"

Sitting forward, she continued her assault before he regrouped his thoughts, an assault directed as much at her libido as at Eric. "I just wished you'd go away. I don't do one-night stands. At least, I never had until that night. If I'd known I'd see you again, I never would have shared a drink with you, much less gone to your hotel room."

How horrible did that admission make her sound?

How much did it brand her Betsy Carmichael's daughter?

Was it even true? No. Eric had made her feel better, made her feel whole. She would have gone anywhere he'd led.

What scared her was that even now, when she was thinking more logically about her mother's death, when she knew she'd slept with a man similar to Randall, Eric still made her feel dazed, made her want to go where he led.

"Then I'm glad you didn't know we'd see each other again." He crossed his arms, his fingers coming so close to touching her she imagined she could feel his body heat sear through her clothes. "I enjoyed making love to you, Kasey."

"I imagine so." She couldn't keep the snideness out of her voice. After all, she'd just compared him to Randall and he was playboy Dr. Douglas's friend. "You should be grateful I left before you woke."

He leaned back, eyed her, his lips twisted with displeasure. "Grateful that you used me for sex and left while I was asleep?"

Was her face as red as it felt?

"Most guys would be grateful to avoid an awkward morning after."

His gaze unwavering, he shrugged. "I'm not most guys."

Yes, she'd noticed that about him.

"The day we met wasn't a good day," she said for lack of knowing what else to say.

"So you've said. Yet you haven't said what was so bad." His voice held a gentle, concerned quality that made her want to squirm.

She didn't want him to be nice. She didn't want to like him, didn't want to believe in the light shining in his eyes that said she could trust him.

Whatever his game was, she wouldn't, *couldn't*, play along. Neither would she.

"What happened to send you into that bar?" Eric asked. "Into my arms?"

Her gaze dropped to the strong arms that had held her so securely. He sounded sincere. It would be so easy to give in, to lean on those broad shoulders.

She knew better, though. Randall had sounded sincere, had let her lean on his shoulders. Then he'd jerked the carpet out from under her feet and trampled on her while she was down.

"My life is none of your business."

Unfazed by her snappish comeback, Eric stared into her eyes. "What if I want to make your life my business? What if I want to see you again because I wasn't grateful you left without waking me?"

Was it even possible? She hadn't thought so, but what if?

Each and every time she'd leaned on another person, she'd fallen. Even if Eric hadn't been grateful she'd left, eventually the attraction would fizzle and then where would she be? Stuck working with an ex. The good-ole-boy system had already driven home how they dealt with sticky situations.

She would not be forced to start over again.

Not even for a man as appealing as Eric.

"I'd say you were out of luck, because the night we met was a fluke and is never going to happen again." She liked her life in Rivendell too much to risk it.

"Kasey," he began, pinning her beneath dark fire.

"Stop right there, Dr. Matthews." She jumped from her seat, refusing to be trapped by his nearness. She held up her hand to ward him off. "What happened between us was a mistake. I don't appreciate you coming to my office, pressuring me this way. I'm not interested. End of story."

He paused, confusion flashing in his eyes. Not backing away, he stayed within inches of her face. "You're serious?"

"Absolutely." Much better to deny the sexual chemistry between her and the fascinating man tempting her to throw caution to the wind. As much as she'd once cared for Randall, he'd never lifted her to the heights this man had in a single night. She might not recover a second time. Not professionally. Not emotionally.

Although Eric looked like he wanted to say more, he clamped his mouth closed and conveyed his displeasure via his tight facial expression.

Resuming his perch on her desk, he watched her for so long she fought to keep standing. His eyes gleamed a deep brown, threatening to burn her with their intensity if she showed the slightest sign of weakness.

His gaze scorched into her soul.

Finally, he gave a curt nod and left.

Kasey's forehead crashed to her desk and she rolled her head back and forth against the hard, cold surface.

Eric was gone.

But he'd be back.

Every workday, he'd be back.

Just how was she going to stay steadfast when confronted with Eric day in and day out?

CHAPTER THREE

A WEEK later, Eric winced at his twenty-year-old patient's bright red skin. "How long were you out in the sun?"

"My boyfriend works on a horse farm and we were out riding. I ended up sticking around and helping him most of the day. Last night I was miserable. I thought I was going to have to go to the emergency room," the young woman admitted, holding her body stiffly.

"I'll be as easy as I can." He gently lifted her loose clothing away from her skin to peer at the burn. "Did you have on sunscreen?"

As impossible as it seemed, her face grew redder. "No. I was working on my tan."

"I'd suggest you work on protecting your skin from permanent damage. A good SPF 30 sunscreen would have saved you a lot of trouble." He motioned toward her burn.

"Oh, you don't have to worry. I've learned my lesson. I plan to go buy the highest SPF in the store."

Eric shook his head. "No need. SPF 30 provides all the protection you need. Once the sun is blocked, it's blocked. Anything beyond just puts extra chemicals on your skin without any real extra protection."

He slipped on his stethoscope and listened to her heart sounds. Normal S1S2 with a regular rate and rhythm. No murmur. Lung sounds clear to auscultation.

"You're losing a lot of moisture through your burn. Make sure you drink a lot of water over the next few days. You want to stay hydrated."

He tapped the RX emblem on the computer screen and entered a prescription for burn cream. He sent the prescription to the pharmacy and printed out a patient education handout on skin care and sunburn.

His next patient was a thin older gentleman with soulful eyes and slumped shoulders. After less than thirty seconds, Eric realized Shane Bresdan needed more than a prescription refill.

The man took a deep breath, stared at his hands. "My wife left."

"Left?"

"Kapooie. She's gone." Shane's tone was flat, as if he talked about the weather. But his eyes held a world of pain and his hands were clenched tightly in his lap.

"Where did she go?"

Sagging shoulders lifted then fell. "Don't know. She just picked up and left while I was at work one day. Came home to a note saying she was gone and wouldn't be back."

And Eric thought he had female problems.

"Were you having marital issues?"

"No more than normal. She's never left before. Never even threatened to."

Poor man. After waking up in his hotel room alone two months ago, Eric wholeheartedly commiserated.

He'd never had a woman walk out on him. He hadn't cared for the experience.

He'd thought he and Kasey had hit it off that night. They had. But whereas he'd gone into the hotel room thinking they were starting something special, she'd gone in thinking of the ending to her bad day.

Eric sighed. Thinking about Kasey was futile when she refused to acknowledge they'd shared anything more than a one-nighter. Was he really such a bad judge of women? Hadn't he learned to read who was sincere and who wasn't? He'd thought so, but perhaps not.

He turned back to his patient. "How are you dealing with her leaving?"

Unpacking his few personal belongings, going along with his mother's constant social demands because it made her happy, and making her happy made him happy, hanging out with Jonathan.

Which had worked until he'd been confronted with the living breathing reminder of the woman who'd bailed out on him.

Now he was discontented as hell.

Eric talked to Shane several more minutes, recommended counseling and an antidepressant. Shane denied suicidal ideas and agreed to return to the clinic for reevaluation. He scheduled a follow-up appointment for a week's time.

Eric shook the man's hand and walked into the hallway with him.

His Kasey radar bleeped. Why was he so aware of a woman who wanted nothing to do with him? He should be grateful. He hadn't come home to start a relationship.

He'd come home for his mother, because he'd heard the need in her voice.

Unable to keep from looking at Kasey, he resigned himself to her reaction. Had four years out of the States really made such a difference in his social skills that he'd gone from fighting off women to chasing after one who denied wanting anything more to do with him? Why didn't he believe her?

She wouldn't have taken off from his hotel room bed if she'd wanted a relationship. Or would she? If she'd known who he was, known they'd be colleagues when he eventually took his place at the clinic, would she have left to throw him off kilter? To leave him wanting more?

He caught her looking at him. Her big green eyes were soulful behind her glasses. Her lower lip was sucked in between her teeth. Her fingers tightly clutched her stethoscope.

Why was she pretending their chemistry didn't exist when it so obviously did?

His gaze roved over the woman standing a few feet away, staring at him with a deer-in-the-headlights expression.

Gold digger or not, he wanted Dr. Kasey Carmichael.

More than he remembered ever wanting a woman.

She wanted him, too.

With time, she'd admit she wanted him.

"How long has your back been hurting, Mr. Oliver?" Kasey asked, making a notation on the sixty-year-old's electronic chart. Mr. Oliver came in every few months with a variety of complaints. Over the time she'd been taking care of him, Kasey had grown fond of the older gentleman, who qualified to come to the ambulatory clinic through a special charity fund sponsored by the Rivendell Ladies Society.

Shoulders covered in dirty coveralls, he shrugged. “On and off for years. Just something I live with, you know. With no insurance, I ain't had much choice.”

Pushing her professional, no-nonsense, black-rimmed glasses up the bridge of her nose, she nodded. Mr. Oliver worked two jobs, trying to support his family. Although his children were all grown, one of his daughters and her three children lived with them. They struggled to make ends meet on the best of days. “When did your back get worse?”

“A couple of weeks ago. I was at work and lifted a car battery. Heard my back pop and then had to have Joe help me straighten.” His weary eyes met hers. “You know Joe. He and his wife come to see you. He drove me here today.”

“Joe's a nice man.” Kasey typed his response into the patient database. “Have you ever had an X-ray of your spine?”

His forehead wrinkled with thought. “Nope. Had one on my shoulder once when I was younger, but that's it.”

Kasey examined his back, running her fingers along his spine, noting the abnormal curvature and areas of spasm. “I'd like to order an X-ray of your lumbar and thoracic spine. That's your low and middle back. You've got some scoliosis that's probably congenital, meaning you were born with it, but I'm concerned you've lost some vertebral height as well.”

"Whatever you say, Doc." He shifted uncomfortably on the exam table. "I'm not sure I can afford X-rays, though."

"They're included in your visit today," she reminded him, glad that cost wouldn't keep Mr. Oliver from getting the care he needed. Yet another reason she volunteered with the Rivendell Ladies Society, a group of Kentucky women who gave back to their community. RLS was the social club, just what she'd dreamed of belonging to while growing up. Kasey's reality had been more along the lines of Public Housing is Us.

Mr. Oliver's brows lifted. "The X-rays are included? I didn't realize."

She nodded, doing her best not to make the proud man feel uncomfortable. She understood he didn't like accepting charity. All too well she understood. Hadn't she once survived on others' charity? Between her booze and her men, Betsy had had little time for her daughter.

No, Kasey wouldn't think of her mother.

To do that would lead to thinking of her death which led to thoughts of meeting Eric. She was having a difficult enough time not thinking of him.

What had his look in the hallway been about? She'd swear when he looked at her he saw right through to her soul. The sensation made her very uncomfortable.

"Have you noticed any burning or tingling in your legs or feet?" she asked her patient, refocusing on the issue at hand.

"No burning, but my feet stay cold. Particularly on the left side." Mr. Oliver lifted the offending foot from the floor, rotating his ankle. She had him flex his foot toward his knee. No pain. Negative Homan's sign.

She indicated for him to take off his shoes. He did so. She took out a sensory tine often used to measure diabetic neuropathy and asked him to tell her when she touched his foot with the bristlelike instrument.

Mr. Oliver had decreased sensation in three of his toes.

She pressed against each toe, closely watching how quickly the nail bed and flesh returned to pink. His capillary refill was within normal limits. Unfortunately, his great toenails bilaterally were yellow, thick and malshaped from a fungal infection. She'd check on pharmaceutical samples. If his liver enzymes came back okay, she'd treat the fungus with an oral medication that would slowly clear the infection. With the decreased sensation, she'd do all she could to protect his feet.

"We may need to do an MRI scan, but I'll wait and see what the X-ray shows." She straightened, filled out an order slip and handed the paper to him. "Take this to the radiology department. It's just beyond the elevators on the right. I've also ordered a urinalysis and a few blood tests that you can stop back by the laboratory in the morning and have done. You need to fast, for at least eight hours before you have the blood drawn so I can check your cholesterol, too."

"Okay." The man stared at the paper in his callused hands. Grease permanently blackened his nails, etched out each and every wrinkle, outlining the story of his life. Years of hard labor as a mechanic couldn't be washed away with soap and water. "Thanks."

Kasey respected Mr. Oliver. Circumstances may have prevented him from having a better life, but he didn't expect handouts, didn't want a free ride.

Unlike her mother.

Despite their monumental differences, Kasey had mourned her mother's death, wished she could have felt more loss over the woman than over what might have been. She couldn't change the past. Her mother was gone and there was no longer hope that someday her mother might get her act together where they could have a real relationship. The relationship they'd had, however lacking, was all they'd ever have.

Kasey bit the inside of her lip to stop the new line of maternal thoughts heading her way. She forced her mother to the recesses of her mind and smiled at her patient.

"When you're done getting the X-rays, stop by the pharmacy, which is one door down from the radiology department. You'll have two prescriptions waiting. One for an anti-inflammatory and one for a muscle relaxant." She told him what the generic prescriptions would cost. "Don't forget to come back as soon as you can for the blood tests, preferably tomorrow. If your labs show anything requiring further treatment, I'll call you."

Gripping his front sheet, he left the exam room. Kasey headed to her office.

Sitting at her desk, she riffled through a stack of papers on her desk, ignoring an announcement of the addition of Dr. Eric Matthews to the ambulatory clinic of Rivendell Medical Center. Instead, she reviewed a cardiology consult letter on Bill Ridner. The words blurred before her eyes. Her mind was filled with the man who haunted her every thought.

The announcement had been sitting on her desk for

a couple of days. Not that she'd let herself read the postcard-sized message. She hadn't. Wouldn't. The less she exposed herself to Eric, the better. The less she knew about the man behind the gorgeous body and quick smile, the better.

An image of that gorgeous body, his passionate kisses while he'd made love to her—had sex with her—caused her to inhale sharply. He'd started at the clinic the day after his surprise arrival a week ago and was working directly with her. How was she supposed to ignore that? Ignore him?

Perhaps she should read the announcement just to learn about her enemy better.

Technically, as head of the ambulatory clinic, she was Eric's superior, but time and again Clive Evans sought out Eric, as did several longtime board members. Had the clinic ever put so much effort into schmoozing a new physician?

The more attention Eric got, the more nervous Kasey became about who would take Herbert's board position.

She rubbed her temple, massaging the dull throb that erupted any time she thought of Eric.

She had a permanent headache these days.

"Okay, so I like him," she admitted to Bones, grimacing at the skeleton on her bookshelf. "A lot."

Way more than she should since a relationship between them was impossible. Could she have picked a worse person to be attracted to? A man who not only was someone she worked with but a doctor who was likely vying for the same promotion she was and had strong family ties to the medical center. Why else would he keep having so many private conversations with the administrator and board members?

He was just like Randall. Rich, spoiled, used to getting what he wanted. When push came to shove, he'd rise to the top, even if he had to step on her to do so. She'd do well to remember that.

Kasey massaged her temple with more vigor, wondering if she'd worn the flesh away from her skull yet. She'd always massaged her temples when she got agitated. At the rate she was going, she was going to look like Bones.

"Kasey?"

She glanced up, barely suppressed a wince at seeing Eric in all his glorious manliness standing in her doorway. As usual, he was dressed impeccably in dark tailored slacks and a crisp button-down shirt.

He stood in her doorway, staring at her. His deep brown eyes told her what his mouth didn't. He wanted her. Probably a case of wanting what he couldn't have, but, regardless, his lingering look sent tingles over her body, flushed her skin, and made her squirm. Hopefully, he hadn't noticed.

Yeah, right. Because he'd gone blind and stupid and hadn't noticed she couldn't keep her eyes off him any time he was near.

"Kasey?" Eric repeated, eyeing her with concern.

"Yes?" She dropped her hand from her temple and inflected as much annoyance into the word as she could. Which was quite a lot since her previous thoughts did annoy her. She didn't want to notice Eric. The only way she'd survive working with him was for her to ignore he existed and for him to ignore her.

Which meant she should probably pray to go blind, deaf and lose all sense of smell.

Because he looked like he'd stepped straight off a Hollywood television set showcasing drop-dead gorgeous doctors, sounded like a Pied Piper's tune that played directly to her dancing libido, smelled so heavenly she wanted to grow wings, wear a halo and learn to play the harp.

So heavenly she was instantly taken back to being wrapped in his arms, their bodies tangled, and breathing in his musk.

Did he possibly have a disorder where he oversecreted pheromones meant to drive women into a heated frenzy?

She'd believe it.

"What do you want?" she bit out tersely, hoping to still her hyperresponsive libido. She didn't need to remember what they'd done, how he'd smiled at her, laced their fingers and— There she went again, remembering what she didn't need to remember.

At her curt question, disappointment flashed across his face, but he didn't comment, just seemed to expect her surliness.

Guilt hit her.

He didn't deserve the way she was treating him.

He'd been nothing but kind to her, and she liked him. So how could she explain that she had to force as much distance between them as possible? That she couldn't afford another blow to her career, but mostly she couldn't deal with how he made her feel weak, like her mother?

To give an inch with Eric would be risking everything she'd worked to achieve. Her pride in herself. Her career.

"I've been with Colin Taylor." His eyes searched hers, piercing her sanity with their intensity. "He usually sees you, but you were booked up this morning, so he scheduled with the new guy instead." His lips lifted in a smile, then paused midway. "Do you have a minute to answer a few questions?"

"In regard to one of my patients? Always."

Even if she did suspect her advice on a patient was the last thing Eric needed. She'd already seen and heard enough to know all accolades regarding his skills were well deserved.

It seemed everyone in the building had something to say about him. She'd very quickly begun blocking out any mention of Eric.

Particularly the rumors that the board planned to ask him, a newcomer, to join their ranks.

"What's going on with Mr. Taylor?" She didn't meet Eric's eyes and, thus, managed to keep her voice level.

"You've scheduled fasting labs for him on three separate occasions, but he never shows. Why is that?"

"Shouldn't you ask Mr. Taylor, rather than me?"

Eric's expression tightened and she rushed on.

"Part of it may be that he doesn't believe the tests are important, despite me telling him otherwise. But it's more likely because he doesn't have a ride to the clinic."

"He doesn't drive?"

"He doesn't own a car. His son usually brings him in for his appointments, but he isn't able to in the mornings."

Eric considered her answer. "How does he get to his job?"

"He walks. About two miles each way."

"Oh." Looking thoughtful, Eric tapped his long fingers against her desk. The methodical rhythm mimicking a subtle attack along the lines of Chinese water torture. Each tap wore on Kasey's sanity.

Instead of caving in, she glared pointedly at the expensive gold watch circling his wrist. "You may have noticed the coding on his billing sheet. Mr. Taylor comes to the clinic through a charity fund provided by the Rivendell Ladies Society." Whom she was to meet with the following evening to discuss their upcoming fundraiser—a masquerade ball. "Not all our clients have padded PPOs. Those who see us through the charity are the working poor and don't have the luxury of dropping everything to follow recommended medical guidelines."

His lips twitched with the hint of a grin reminiscent of the ones he'd flashed at Calista Blue's. Her breath caught.

"Feel that strongly about it, do you?"

Her and her big mouth. She'd gotten up on her soapbox and said too much. Had she expected him to become defensive? To argue with her? Had she hoped he was an elitist snob so she could hold it against him? No one knew she'd grown up in the poorest area of Lexington, that if not for government assistance programs and charity, she'd have been homeless, starved.

"I suppose." She didn't elaborate, just went back to studying Bill Ridner's cardiology report. "It's my job to care about my patients."

He crossed his arms and regarded her. "Why is it that no matter what I say, it's the wrong thing? What's changed from the night we met? I'd have sworn you liked me that night, that we had a connection."

"You know what changed," she answered honestly. "We were never meant to see each other after that night. The fact we now work together makes the situation awkward."

"You're right about the situation being awkward, but it doesn't have to be." His eyes sparkled like dark amber. "I'm interested in you. You aren't interested in me. Fine." He shrugged. "Forget that I want to make love to you until you can't see straight. Let's be friends."

Friends? They couldn't be friends. A friend didn't battle urges to run her fingers over broad shoulders. A friend wouldn't be so acutely aware of how his pulse beat at the base of his throat, of how when he smiled a dimple dug into his right cheek. A friend's body didn't explode with pleasure when he— *Friends?* Was he insane? They couldn't be friends.

She wouldn't even touch his "Forget that I want to make love to you until you can't see straight." Like a woman could forget when a sexy man told her that and she knew he had the skills to back up his claim.

"Why would you want us to be friends?" Had her voice squeaked?

His gaze didn't waver, just continued to probe further and further inside her. "I like you."

"You like me?" Why did she hold her breath while waiting for his answer? Lord, she was losing it.

All because of the man standing before her and his irresistible appeal. He wanted to make love to her again. Because he couldn't have her. Everything about Eric said he wasn't used to being told no.

He smiled self-derisively, as if he couldn't help himself for being sexy, as if he couldn't help that he made her want to run straight into the blade of a broken heart.

He probably couldn't.

"I made my feelings apparent on the night we met," he clarified. "Nothing's changed on my part."

Heat crept into Kasey's cheeks. Out of habit she pushed against her glasses, sliding them up as far as they'd go on the bridge of her nose. "You were drunk the night we met."

"You think so?" His dark brow arched, his expression somber. "There wasn't any alcohol in my soda, Kasey."

There hadn't been? "It doesn't matter. We can't be friends."

His forehead wrinkled. "Why not?"

Because he made her want to forgo a lifetime of promises that she wouldn't be like her mother. With Randall, she'd been naïve, believed they'd end up married with a house in an upscale neighborhood, send their kids to the right schools, and grow old together. In the end, she hadn't been good enough for anything beyond sex. He'd married the blue-blooded daughter of one of Skymont's trustees.

She suspected Eric's background made Randall look like a poor ole boy. In the long run, Eric would want someone like him, someone who came from wealth and prestige and good stock. No matter how far Kasey had come, how proud she was of her success and the woman she'd become, she was still poor little Kasey Carmichael from the wrong side of town. She was still the daughter of Betsy Carmichael who'd had a revolving door to her bedroom and a predilection for alcohol.

Kasey bit the inside of her lip and wondered how they'd gone from discussing Mr. Taylor to a conversation about the night they'd met. Discussing work was much safer.

"You were asking about Mr. Taylor?" she reminded him, hoping her voice conveyed that she was no longer willing to discuss anything personal. "Was there something specific you needed to know regarding his care?"

Eric sighed, but let her change the subject back to their patient. "I'm concerned we're missing something. His MRI showed degenerative disc disease. He certainly has symptoms from his back issues, but I'm worried more is going on."

She tried not to let his "we're missing something" comment irk. Since this was his first time seeing Mr. Taylor, what he really meant was that she was missing something. "More?"

"His prostate is enlarged."

Around fifty percent of men over the age of fifty had an enlarged prostate. Kasey stared, waiting for him to say something more enlightening.

"Did he tell you that his father and grandfather both had prostate cancer in their early sixties?"

Mr. Taylor hadn't told her and she'd taken a detailed family history from him on several occasions. Had repeatedly examined him without him mentioning urinary symptoms, erectile dysfunction or symptoms that had made her suspect prostate issues. He'd had a digital rectal exam not long after she'd first seen him at the clinic, but she couldn't recall just how long ago that had been. Eric had apparently done another today since he'd said Mr. Taylor's prostate was enlarged. Had she missed something important on one of her patients?

"I want to get a prostate specific antigen on him as soon as possible. I tried to get him to go to the lab today, but he thought he should wait and do the labs you'd ordered."

"In addition to the comprehensive metabolic profile, complete blood count and cholesterol panel, I ordered a PSA, too. If you read my notes, you saw that I've encouraged him to have the labs drawn while here, even though it meant forgoing the lipid check. He's repeatedly refused." Was he criticizing her skills? Would he twist the care she'd provided to Mr. Taylor in an attempt to make her look incompetent to the board? "Why are you telling me this?"

Eric eyed her, clearly not understanding her hostile tone. "He's your patient."

"He saw you today," she spat out. Did she sound petty? She hadn't meant to, but Eric made her antsy. Among other things.

"Yes, but you know him better than I do. He mentions you with every other breath," Eric pointed out. "He knows you're an excellent doctor, and he trusts your opinion. I thought you could talk to him, convince him to have the PSA drawn even if he isn't prepared to have the other tests."

He was legitimately concerned for their patient.

Eric didn't deserve how she was treating him. Not personally, not professionally. She had to find a balance between keeping him at a distance and being so prickly.

For that matter, she'd felt prickly and emotionally wrought from the moment Eric had arrived on the scene.

She blamed her mother's death, but also her unexpected reaction to Eric and the fact she couldn't get him out of her head no matter how much she tried.

Looking into Eric's concerned brown eyes, she couldn't recall why she even wanted to get him out of her head.

What she wanted was to tell him she was sorry, to tell him that he made her want things she was afraid of wanting because the last time she'd let herself have those dreams she'd gotten badly burned.

That she'd been embarrassed she'd slept with him on the night they'd met.

That looking at him, wanting him, made her feel like the little girl she'd once been with her nose smashed against a store window, eyeing the goodies inside.

"If he schedules with me," she started over, making sure to keep her voice polite, professional, not prickly, "I'll talk with him. But if it's regarding his prostate, he's just as likely to schedule with you or Dr. Douglas."

Several of her regular male patients saw Dr. Douglas when the time came to have certain male body parts checked. Vice versa, too. She and Grace, the clinic's nurse practitioner, saw some of Dr. Douglas's patients for their female problems, but at no other time.

"Okay." Eric lingered for several more minutes without speaking, as if he was waiting for her to say something.

What? she wanted to scream.

Instead, she went back to doing what she'd been attempting to do for weeks. She ignored him. Or pretended to. Which was the crux of what she'd been doing.

"Kasey?"

Heart pounding, she looked up, fought gulping back

the ball of emotions clogging her throat. "Is there something else?"

"Yes."

Her pulse leaped, her breath caught, her hands clasped together to keep them from nervously fluttering around while she waited for him to make his move.

And waited.

Because he just sat across from her, watching her with an intensity that made her think he was committing every feature to memory. That he wanted her to act on the strong impulse within her to go to him, bury her fingers into his dark hair and pull him to her lips.

What was it Eric wanted of her? Just sex?

Because she was smart enough to recognize that all he had to do was touch her and she'd go up in flames, would likely beg him to make love to her again. He recognized that truth, too. But he didn't press his advantage, which totally confused her.

And frustrated her.

Dear heavens, did she want him to press?

He let out an exasperated sigh. "I'm not going anywhere, Kasey. Which means that eventually you're going to have to deal with what happened between us. What's going to happen between us." He leaned forward, hovering inches from her face.

Her gaze dropped from his expressive eyes to his mouth. Kasey gulped.

"For the record—" his pupils darkened to almost black "—I'm not talking about wanting to be your friend."

CHAPTER FOUR

"DO YOU want to talk about it?" Jonathan asked later that night at the Calista Blue bar where Eric had met him for dinner and to catch a televised baseball game.

The bar where Eric had met Kasey.

He and Jonathan had gotten drinks and ordered their food. Flashing a flirty smile, their waitress placed their order on the table.

"Nope." Eric took a drink of his soda. He rarely drank alcohol these days and never when he was upset.

Kasey upset him. In a big way.

Why did he get the feeling that every time she pushed him away, she was really running from herself?

"There are a million girls in this town who would love to take your mind off Kasey Carmichael." Jonathan took a swig from his longneck. "Like those two hottie blondes over there."

Not acknowledging his friend's mention of Kasey, Eric followed his gaze. Sure enough, two women were giving them come-hither looks. Once upon a time, he might have been interested, but he hadn't had a fling in over four years.

During his mission work, he'd had two committed relationships, one with an Australian doctor who'd volunteered with the group for a year and the other with the daughter of a British diplomat who'd funded the vaccination program Eric had helped implement. Later, he'd learned both had known who he was, his family connections. Just as well that he hadn't been under any illusions that either relationship would lead to marriage.

In his heart, he'd always known he'd go back to Kentucky and find a balance between the life his heritage demanded of him and the life he wanted for himself.

Eric motioned toward the smiling women. "Go ahead. I'm not interested."

Jonathan's jaw dropped. "You can't be serious?"

"I don't need you to start matchmaking, too," Eric snapped.

Jonathan shook his head. "Ouch. Somebody sure is testy."

Knowing his friend was right, Eric grimaced. "Sorry."

"It's your mother doing the matchmaking?" Jonathan took a drink. "Or do I want to ask?"

"Probably not." Eric inhaled a deep breath. "And, yes, it's my mother. Despite my insistence that I'm not interested, she's setting me up with one of her cronies' daughters. Not that she calls them dates. They're 'social functions'."

Jonathan laughed. "And you aren't interested in these social functions."

"No."

"Because you're interested in a particular coworker of ours."

Eric didn't answer.

Jonathan eyed him a minute before saying, "You should go to Aruba with me tomorrow. The sun and babes will take your mind off the Ice Queen."

Glaring at Jonathan's use of the nickname, Eric shook his head. "I've only been on the job a week. I can't take off for Aruba." Once he would have taken up the offer without a thought to his responsibilities, without a care in the world. That had been a long time ago. "If you'd wanted to do Aruba together, we should have gone before I started at the clinic."

Eric stared at his friend's amused expression. "Besides, I didn't say I was thinking about Kasey."

"You didn't have to," Jonathan snorted. "The entire office knows you have the hots for her. Probably the entire building. Why haven't you asked her out on a date?"

"Good question and one I wished I knew the answer to." He needed time with her, time to explore the uncharted emotional waters he was currently drowning in. "She won't have me."

Taking a sip of his beer, Jonathan grunted. "She had you on the night you met."

"I never said that," Eric replied. He'd been very closemouthed about the night he and Kasey had met. A few times he'd wondered if Jonathan could shed some light on where he'd gone wrong with Kasey. But as good a person as Jonathan was, he'd have agreed with Kasey about being grateful she'd left without waking him. To Jonathan, that would have been the perfect night. Phenomenal sex with no strings attached.

"You didn't have to." His friend stuck a fried pickle

in his mouth. "The Ice Queen gave you brain freeze and now you're warped."

"Apparently, and I told you not to call her that."

Not looking in the slightest reprimanded, Jonathan grinned. "No worries, pal. I've seen how she looks at you. She's got the same warped brain disease you do." Jonathan lifted his beer in salute. "Go get healed together or something."

Right. All he had to do was convince Kasey. Piece of cake.

"It's not that simple."

"Of course it is. You want her. She wants you." Jonathan shrugged. "Just make your sleek Eric Matthews move and reel her in."

His sleek Eric Matthews move? Had he ever had such a move? He'd never had to work for a woman. He wasn't even sure he knew how. Maybe that's what he was doing wrong.

"You weren't paying attention," he admonished. "I've already made my move. She turned me down flat."

Jonathan almost choked on his appetizer. "You're kidding?"

"I wish."

Jonathan threw his head back in laughter. "I never thought I'd see the day when a chick shot you down."

"Yeah, well, you have now."

Jonathan took a swig of his beer, then shrugged. "Maybe you should count yourself lucky. Kasey's all about her career. It's no secret her sights are set on the board."

"How do you know that?"

"Advancement is a big deal to her. Honestly, it's surprised me that she's stayed in the ambulatory clinic as that isn't the most politically advantageous spot to work within the facility." Jonathan shot him a look. "At least, it wasn't until Lena Matthews's son took an interest in the clinic."

"So, why is Kasey still in the ambulatory clinic if she's all about her career?"

"The only thing I can figure is that she honestly believes in the charity fund's work."

After her heartfelt defense of the fund, Eric could believe that.

"I know you've not made a big deal of who you are, but does she know?"

Eric shrugged. "I'm not sure. I didn't think so, but sometimes I wonder."

"You think that's why she hooked up with you that night?"

"I didn't say we hooked up. But I will admit that if it had been Kasey who'd invited me to Aruba, I'd be packing my bags."

Grinning, Jonathan held his hand over his heart. "I'm crushed."

Eric laughed. "Yeah, I can tell."

The waitress put their food in front of them just as a cheer went up around the bar. Someone had just knocked a home run.

Eyeing the television monitor closest to them, they dug into their food and for a few hours Eric forgot about Kasey Carmichael.

* * *

The following Monday, Kasey handed Lora a lab request for a patient she'd spoken with on the phone. "Thanks."

"You're welcome." A pretty pink blossomed in the blonde's cheeks. "We got a postcard from Dr. Douglas today."

Kasey blinked in surprise. *Dr. Douglas had sent a postcard?*

"That's nice," she said for lack of knowing what to say. Dr. Douglas didn't seem like the postcard-sending type. Had he ever sent a note before during one of his frequent vacations?

Perhaps the card was in Eric's honor.

"He says Aruba is awesome, and he wishes we were there." Lora sounded wistful, as if she wished she was there. For the view or for Dr. Douglas, Kasey wasn't sure. Lora had been one of the many women to go through the revolving door of Dr. Douglas's life. Kasey hadn't ever been convinced the nurse had gotten over him.

"Aruba sounds fairly tempting after the last two patients we've seen this morning." A bipolar patient who'd gone off her medications and another in for the removal of an ingrown toenail. The removal of toenails was one of Kasey's pet peeves. She'd yet to do one where her own toenails didn't curl tightly into her shoes.

"Tell me about it. Give me the sun, a beach and a good book and I'm so there," Lora mused, turning when an exam-room door opened behind her.

Eric stepped into the hallway, a serious look on his face. Usually his eyes twinkled, but no merriment danced in his deep brown gaze now. Not that Kasey was looking *that* closely.

"Just who I was needing." He was looking at her, too. That closely. "Can we talk a minute?" At her obvious hesitation, he gave an exasperated sigh and added, "Regarding the patient I'm currently seeing."

A room that had been used for storage on the opposite side of Dr. Douglas's office was being renovated for Eric. Currently, the two men were sharing Dr. Douglas's office. Whereas Kasey's office was tidy and trendy, Dr. Douglas's was crammed full of books, medical magazines, sports memorabilia and various educational wall posters sponsored by pharmaceutical companies.

Kasey followed Eric, turning suspicious when he closed the door. However, his expression remained somber, piquing her curiosity.

"I'm with Maggie Payne," he began. He stood in front of the overflowing desk, arms crossed, staring expectantly at her. "Do you recall who she is?"

"Yes." A too-thin woman with sad eyes came to mind. "I've seen her a few times over the past couple of months. Isn't she a construction worker?"

"So she says." His tone disbelieving, he blew out a frustrated breath. "You last saw her for injuries resulting from a fall off a ladder. I'm seeing her today for trauma from a roof beam giving way."

Immediately, Kasey knew what he was getting at. One accident could be written off, but two major accidents in such a short time was suspicious for abuse. Heat dampened her body, making her palms clammy. "Perhaps she's just unlucky."

"Perhaps she's being abused and is covering for the bastard." His face red, Eric's hands clenched at his sides.

Kasey's stomach knotted into a tight ball. "Did you ask her?"

"She insists no one hit her, but her bruises indicate otherwise."

Kasey took a few deep breaths, forced her voice to remain steady. "You can report your findings to the police, but if she denies it and won't press charges, there's nothing we can do."

Looking pensive, he nodded. "You should talk to her."

"Me?" she squeaked, feeling light-headed. "Why me?"

Did he somehow sense her past? Somehow see right through her to the life she'd desperately put behind her?

"Because you're a woman."

Her nerve endings sizzled throughout her body. "What does that have to do with anything?"

"I'm a man, and she probably sees me as the enemy. As a woman, she might open up to you."

For many reasons, Kasey hated dealing with abuse cases. She understood her phobias, understood the whys, but understanding didn't make her job any easier. She always made sure her patients were taken good care of, but she referred abuse cases out fast.

The thought of confronting Maggie made her feel squeamish.

"Okay," she agreed hesitantly. "If you think it'll make a difference."

"If I didn't, I wouldn't have asked," he said, staring oddly at her.

Battling personal demons, Kasey followed him into the exam room and tried to keep from wincing at the woman's black eye and swollen upper lip. She was dressed in a hospital gown and through the gaps deep purple bruises marred Maggie's ribs. More could be seen on her upper arms. Like someone had grabbed her, shaken her. Fading yellow-green bruises dotted her thin body.

Eric was right. Maggie hadn't fallen from a roof and although her injuries hadn't been nearly so severe or clear-cut, she likely hadn't fallen from a ladder before her last visit.

"Maggie, you've met Dr. Carmichael," he said in such a gentle voice that Kasey was pulled from her thoughts and looked at him. His face shone with compassion. "I thought, under the circumstances, you might be more comfortable if she examines you."

Tearing her eyes away from Eric, Kasey looked at the woman to see if she, too, had been moved by his sincerity. If the woman found herself wanting to lean on him and pour out her heart.

"Look." Frustration shone in Maggie's eyes. "It really doesn't matter who examines me. I fell from a roof. I just came to the clinic because it hurts to breathe."

Eric met Kasey's gaze. "She'll probably need a chest X-ray."

Unable to stand the intensity in his eyes or the way her heart sped up in response to that intensity, Kasey patted Maggie's hand. "Dr. Matthews is going to leave so I can examine you. We'll talk woman to woman while he's gone."

Eric took the hint and left the room.

Kasey examined the woman, battled tears at the extent of her injuries, battled tears that always threatened when confronted with abuse. Tears from the past.

"Maggie," she began. "I know you told Dr. Matthews that you fell, but that's not what happened. If you don't want to report who did this to you, that's your choice, but my choice is your safety."

"What about my choices?" Maggie shivered, shaking her head back and forth in denial. "If you tell the police, he'll kill me."

"Who?" Kasey asked gently.

"My old man. He only gets mean when he drinks," Maggie said defensively.

"Then he needs to quit drinking."

"Tell me about it." The woman sighed, then whimpered in pain at Kasey's touch. "He busted me up pretty bad this time, didn't he?"

"Yes." She continued her exam, being as gentle as possible. "I can't feel any displaced ribs, but that doesn't mean there aren't fractures. Did he kick you?"

Kasey continued talking with Maggie, examining her, documenting objective findings and asking questions, becoming more and more emotionally involved in the woman's plight.

"I can't leave him. I love him," Maggie sobbed.

"Loving someone doesn't mean you have to stay in an abusive relationship. Taking a stand that this is wrong doesn't lessen your love."

Maggie's head lowered. "Someone like you can't understand."

"I understand better than you think." Kasey took a deep breath. She'd treated abuse cases before, but this was the first time she'd spoken of her shameful past out loud. She ignored the voice asking, *Why now?* "My mother was an alcoholic and a mean drunk, too. I grew up having a lot of *accidents*."

So many that the state had stepped in several times to remove her from her mother's care. Somehow Betsy had always managed to straighten up long enough to regain custody. Until the next time.

"I was ashamed to admit to anyone that my own mother would do such things to me. I even remember thinking that perhaps I deserved the way she treated me. As soon as I was old enough to know better, to take care of myself, I left because no one deserves to be treated this way." She gave a pointed look at Maggie's bruises. "Being under the influence doesn't make hitting another person okay."

Maggie stared at her, surprise at Kasey's admission shining in her eyes. "You think I don't know it's not okay? I know that. That doesn't mean I can leave. Where would I go? I can't support myself. I didn't even graduate from high school."

Abusers often convinced their victims of their inability to get by without them, cutting them off from all sources of support. It was all part of the abuse, all part of how they kept the victim under their thumb. As a child, Kasey hadn't had a choice. This woman had choices.

"I can call someone to help you, Maggie. Someone who will give you a place to stay and help keep you safe. What your boyfriend is doing is wrong. He needs help. If you allow this to continue…" she indicated the bruises on the woman's body "…you're not helping him or yourself. I know it isn't easy, but nothing worthwhile is. I made myself a better life. So can you."

Kasey heard a noise behind her, turned and saw Eric standing just inside the door. Her lips parted, but nothing came out.

How long had he been standing there?

How much had he heard?

The soft glow in his sympathetic eyes said he'd heard too much.

Although she'd never revealed the cause of her tears, she'd cried in his arms on the night they'd met, grieving over her mother's death. Now Eric knew her deepest, darkest secret. What next?

She didn't want him to *know* her, to look at her and see beneath the polished surface she'd spent years perfecting.

Most definitely she didn't want his pity.

Sensing Kasey's discomfort, Eric fought his own unease.

She'd been abused as a child.

Fury like none he'd known, not even during the most unjust conditions he'd been exposed to while in Africa, stormed his chest. Fury that Kasey's mother had hurt her, betrayed the trust a child so innocently gave to a parent.

"I, uh…" Kasey looked flummoxed, but as if she was trying to stay calm. Her eyes held the same panicked look as on the day he'd shown up at the office. "I'll order X-rays, Maggie. And a blood count just to be sure your levels don't indicate internal bleeding."

She gave a nervous laugh, totally inappropriate and a sign of how upset she was that he'd overheard her conversation.

Damn it, why wouldn't she let him in? She had on that one night. She'd said she had a bad day. Had something happened with her mother? Was that what had upset her so much she'd come to that bar and found him?

Part of him had wondered about her motives for spending the night with him, for leaving before he'd awakened. But more and more he suspected her reasons had had nothing to do with him, nothing to do with who he was, and everything to do with Kasey and who she was beneath all the layers she'd carefully constructed.

"Think about what I said, Maggie," she said with one last comforting touch to the woman's hand. "You can make a better life for yourself."

With that Kasey pushed past him, obviously expecting him to stay with Maggie. Instead, he excused himself and followed Kasey out of Maggie's room and into an empty exam room. Her head was in her hands.

Was she crying?

"Kasey?"

She turned, eyes flashing with tears. "You had no right to eavesdrop."

"I wasn't eavesdropping." But he had been. "At least, not intentionally," he corrected. "I did knock before opening the door."

He stepped toward her, his spirits lifting when she didn't back away. "I'm sorry about your mother, Kasey."

Her eyes narrowed into tiny slits. "Don't tell me you're sorry when you know nothing."

"I'd like to know," he admitted, closing the distance between them. "Let me know you, Kasey."

"No." She bit into her lip. "No." A tear slid down her cheek. "No. No. No."

Not letting her push him away, he wrapped his arms around her and pulled her close. Feeling inadequate, he held her, planning to let her cry. "Shh, it's okay."

It would be okay, because he'd protect her from the world. Always. Even as he thought it, he recognized that he should be afraid, more afraid than he'd ever been, but he wasn't.

He'd come home for a reason. He'd thought it was his mother. To honor the family legacy he'd once scorned.

Now he wondered if he'd come home for a woman he'd never met.

A woman who reached places he hadn't known existed inside him.

The next day, Kasey saw an upper respiratory infection patient and refilled another patient's hypertension medications. Another three patients and she'd caught up for the morning, but the receptionist registered two more drop-ins.

"Sorry, Kasey," Lora said, "but Agnes couldn't bear to turn them away."

"No problem. She's good at screening who can wait and who can't. I'll see them."

She didn't want a single moment's downtime. Not when she'd made such a fool of herself following her consult with Maggie yesterday. Thoughts of how she'd once again cried in Eric's arms receded to the back of her mind when she was with patients.

Thank God she'd managed to avoid him the rest of the day.

"Do you want me to have them come back after lunch?" Lora asked.

Kasey shook her head. "There's no reason for them to wait that long. I'd rather go ahead and see them now."

She needed all the distractions she could get, because her brain seemed to be on a single track these days.

As if her thoughts had conjured him up, Eric stepped out of an exam room. "I'll take one of the patients so Kasey will have time for lunch."

She started to deny him, say that she'd see both, but when their eyes met, she just nodded.

There was an odd light in his eyes. A light she'd seen in his eyes yesterday when he'd held her after her encounter with Maggie. A light that warned change was in the air. Hah, change had been in the air since the night she'd met him.

When Kasey had finished examining her late arrival, she saw the gentleman, almost crippled with rheumatoid arthritis, to the front of the clinic. She turned to go to her office to grab her purse. Eric stood directly in her path.

Had he been waiting on her to finish?

"I think I got the easy patient. She only needed a medication refill." He grinned, but his eyes searched her face. As if he was worried about her, as if he, too, kept thinking of yesterday. "Are you headed to lunch?"

Wanting to get away from his penetrating gaze, she absently nodded.

"Great. Me, too." Smiling, he took a step toward her. "We'll go together."

No way did she want to go to lunch with him.

"You go ahead." Had her voice gone up an octave? "I'm not going to the clinic's restaurant."

The bottom floor of the clinic boasted a small in-house cafeteria that served a variety of menu options. Most of their coworkers and a few of their patients would be dining there. Unfortunately, they didn't serve organic, but a small privately owned café a couple of blocks away did.

"Even better." A self-satisfied smile curved his lips and his eyes sparkled so intently she took a step back. "Let's go. On the way there I can tell you about what Colin Taylor's tests showed."

She couldn't think of a single reason why she could say no without looking petty in front of Lora, who'd stepped into the hallway. Or perhaps she couldn't think period.

Not with Eric looking at her that way.

A way that had Lora glancing back and forth between them. Oh, yeah, her nurse was curious.

No wonder. All the staff adored him, especially the women. They went out of their way to chat with him, to fetch this or that for him, to bat their eyelashes at him. Not Kasey. She'd intentionally have walked on nails to keep from bumping into him.

However, minutes later she was nestled into the front seat of Eric's expensive sedan and soaked in the mixture of fine leather and even finer man.

God, was it so wrong that she wanted to be with him?

Even if she could only do so in a professional capacity?

"Nice car."

He glanced around as if noticing his vehicle for the first time. "It's a ride."

The car looked brand-new. Not a spec of dust anywhere and no way could you fake that new-car smell. "Oh?"

"It was a coming-home gift from my mother, but not

what I usually drive," he admitted, giving her a sideways glance. "My truck is in the shop, getting a tune-up."

A gift from his mother. What kind of mother gave a luxury car for a "coming home" gift?

"You drive a truck?" She shouldn't ask, shouldn't care, but he'd piqued her curiosity.

"An SUV, actually." Eric glanced at her and shrugged, oblivious to her inner turmoil. "It's what I drove before I left the States. I like it. Lots of room to haul stuff—or unsuspecting women." He waggled his brows at the last, then put his attention back on the road. "Something I can get muddy, pull a horse trailer with or take a date to a nice restaurant."

Muddy. She had a difficult time picturing Eric muddy, but no doubt he'd look great coated in mud.

She swallowed the lump that formed in her throat.

He parked his car outside the restaurant. She glanced at him in surprise. He'd driven straight to Barnaby's.

"Eat here often?" She headed here most days that she could get away from the clinic, but rarely did she see any of her colleagues. Never had she seen Eric. She definitely would have noticed if he'd been anywhere in the vicinity.

"No," he continued, oblivious to her thoughts, "but I've been meaning to try it. Jonathan mentioned you ate organic so I figured this was where you were headed. I hear the food's good."

Kasey's insides tingled. "You and Dr. Douglas talk about my eating preferences?"

Not seeming in the slightest ashamed at his admission, Eric pocketed his keys.

"I asked about you. He told me what little he knows." He ran his palm over the buttery leather of the steering wheel, then turned toward her, his face sincere. "I'll say this again in case you've somehow misunderstood. I can't stop thinking about you and want to know everything about you."

He looked at her as if she were flawless, an enthralled look that made her feel…priceless.

Which was utterly ridiculous.

She rolled her eyes and got out of the car before she said something she shouldn't. Like that she couldn't stop thinking about him, too, and what were they going to do about it?

The restaurant was crowded. Kasey thought she'd glimpsed a member of the Rivendell Ladies Society leaving when they'd first arrived, but otherwise she didn't see anyone she knew.

Which was probably good since she was dining with Eric.

By the end of the meal, she felt equally flustered and flushed with excitement.

Life was lonely when you'd become afraid to let anyone close to you for fear of disappointment and pain. Yet she'd never been close to anyone who didn't eventually disappoint and hurt her.

For one night, she had let Eric close.

She'd felt alive. When she looked at him, she felt electrified. Aware of every breath she took. Aware of every cell in her body.

He did that to her.

She met his intent gaze.

Deep in her heart she wanted to give him a chance to prove he wasn't like Randall, wasn't like the men who'd come and gone from her mother's life.

But if she gave him that chance, would he only end up breaking her heart and quite possibly destroying her career?

A scenario that was all too likely to happen.

Yet could she live with the knowledge that she'd let the fear of failure trap her inside a glass box of her own making?

Eric leaned back in his chair, watching emotion after emotion flash across Kasey's beautiful face. Each day he found something to ask her, some way of spending a few moments with her, knowing that eventually he'd wear down the wall she'd erected.

Yesterday, as he'd held her, a few chunks had fallen away from that protective wall.

What would she do if he leaned across the table and kissed her? Probably slap him. The chunks hadn't been that big.

Still, she needed a little shaking up.

Or was that what had happened that night?

"You never told me what upset you the day we met."

"Didn't I?" she answered vaguely, taking another sip of her water, not glancing his way. Her cheeks held a high glow, as if she was overly warm.

"What happened to cause you to come to that bar and order a beer when you obviously don't drink?" he pushed, giving her that shake. Did her reasons have to do with what she'd told Maggie yesterday?

Kasey stared at her fork as if the tines held the formula to cure all man's afflictions. "Why?"

Because that night she'd liked him, wanted him, clung to him. "I want to understand you."

"Why would you want to do that?"

Because he wanted her to like him again, to want him again, to cling to him again. "Why wouldn't I? We're friends."

"No," she denied, with a low laugh. "We're not. Otherwise you wouldn't have said you want to be friends. That implies we aren't friends."

"Fine." He exhaled a deep sigh. "We're not friends, but we are coworkers. Coworkers are allowed to be concerned about one another."

"Rivendell employs hundreds of people. I don't share my personal information with them."

"Okay." Tiring of whatever game she played, he went for broke. "We're more than coworkers, more than friends, and whether you admit it or not, you know we would be lots more if you weren't so stubborn."

Her eyes flashed green sparks. "What would we be if I weren't so stubborn?"

"Lovers."

She swallowed. "We can't be lovers. We work together."

He arched a brow. An interesting denial. "Technically, we already are."

Her cheeks glowed a bright shade of pink. "One night doesn't make us lovers."

"Perhaps not," he admitted, staring directly into her

eyes. "But I've dreamed of making love to you every night since we met. That should count for something."

"Face it." She swallowed again, her voice low, steady. Surprisingly, she didn't look away, didn't try to hide the swirling desire in her eyes. "You only want me because I've not fallen at your feet."

"I'm willing to test that theory, Kasey." Placing his palms flat against the table, he leaned forward. "Fall at my feet."

She hesitated for the briefest moment. "I can't fall at your feet. It would hurt my career."

Eric frowned. Dating him would hurt her career? Surely she didn't believe that. He was striking out with Kasey for the very reason people usually wanted to be with him. Her comment struck him as ironic. Did she think if things didn't work he'd hurt her professionally? That stung.

"You won't date me because we work together?" He pinned her with his gaze, refused her the right to look away. "That's the reason you keep saying no?"

Pensive, she nodded. "It's a reason."

Finally they were getting somewhere. "Let's say we didn't work together, then what? Would getting rid of working together be enough for you to go out with me?"

She hesitated, then inhaled sharply. "Yes."

Eric mentally high-fived himself. "Fine. I'll give my notice when we get back to the office. How does dinner at six-thirty sound?"

Kasey's eyes widened, her jaw dropped, and she stared at him as if he'd lost his mind. Then a wide smile spread across her face and she burst out laughing. "You're crazy."

"So it would seem." He smiled back, lifted his glass and saluted her. "About you."

Her full lips stilled, curved. She shook her head. "What am I going to do about you?"

"Let me show you why you should have said yes all along," he suggested, knowing from the glow in her eyes that he had her. Whatever had been holding her back had shifted. She'd quit fighting the chemistry sparking between them.

She pursed her lips. "Lunch isn't enough?"

"Not by far." He swept his gave over her face, settling on her mouth. "Just so you're prewarned, dinner won't be enough either. I've missed you."

"Dinner will have to be enough," she informed him, her eyes shining with a glow he hadn't seen before. "I'm not going to sleep with you, Eric."

"I've heard that before," he teased. "A few hours later, I'm trying to play the role of the gentleman and you beg me to—"

She wadded up her napkin and tossed the paper at him. "You'd have to play the role. You're no gentleman."

No, much to his mother's disappointment, he never had been. "You can't blame a guy for trying."

"Oh, I blame you all right. I blame you for all of this." Although she smiled and the twinkle still glowed in her eyes, there was a heavy dose of reality in her words.

"What do you blame on me, Kasey?"

"I wasn't looking to meet anyone on the night we met," she admitted, her gaze downcast at her water glass. "I was in that bar to keep from being alone, but I wasn't looking for what happened or for a relationship."

"But we did meet." He reached across the table, laid his hand over hers. "I'm glad we met, that we happened. We were good together."

"You've complicated my life in ways you don't even begin to understand," she said, seeming to carefully measure each word.

"You think I like being caught up in a woman who doesn't want anything to do with me?" He stared straight into her eyes and refused to let her look away, refused to let her wiggle her hand out from under his. "I am caught up, Kasey. Crazy caught up. What happened the day we met?"

"My mother's funeral."

CHAPTER FIVE

"YOUR mother died?" Eric's heart lurched in his chest, pounding against his rib cage.

"Well, I didn't bury her alive, if that's what you're thinking." Face pale, she squeezed her eyes shut, regret at her admission evident.

She hadn't meant to tell him, hadn't meant to share her grief.

Her mother's funeral. That explained the tears on the night they'd met.

"Why didn't you tell me? Why would you keep that to yourself?" Damn it, why had she pushed him away when he could have been there? She shouldn't have had to grieve alone. "Why didn't Jonathan tell me about your mother when I asked him about you?"

"When I took off work to go to Lexington, I didn't tell anyone I was going to my mother's funeral. Just that something unexpected had come up and I needed time off work a few days." Her gaze dropped to where he held her hand, his fingers clutching her trembling ones.

Eric let her softly spoken admission register. She'd

admitted to Maggie that she'd left home as a teenager. Had she seen her abusive mother since?

"She'd had liver disease for a long time," she continued. "The medical examiner's report said she died from liver failure."

Clearly, the news had left her devastated.

So devastated she'd spent the night with him.

"We weren't close, but her death shocked me. I guess death shocks everyone." She closed her eyes and took a deep breath. When her eyes opened, raw pain shone in the green depths. "I never wanted her dead, Eric."

Not caring who in the restaurant saw, Eric lifted her hand and kissed her fingertips. "Sometimes things happen and we don't understand the reasons."

No wonder she'd looked distraught when she'd sat down next to him. No wonder she'd cried while he'd held her. As interfering as his mother was, he loved her dearly and couldn't imagine not having her meddling in his life. Even while he'd been in Africa, she'd always let him know he was loved, missed.

"I hadn't seen her for almost two years," Kasey admitted, swiping at her eyes with an embarrassed glance around the restaurant. She needn't have bothered. No one paid them any attention.

He stroked his thumb across her hand, marveling at how soft she felt when he knew what strength lay in her capable touch.

"When I left the funeral home, I felt so alone. She was the only family I had and she was gone. With her death went all my dreams that someday she'd sober up and we could be a real family. As I drove home from

Lexington, all I could think was that I didn't want to be alone." Sadness filled her eyes. "Still, I shouldn't have picked up a stranger in a bar."

"You didn't pick up a stranger." He laced their fingers and gave a squeeze. "You picked me."

Her eyes glimmering with tears, she shook her head. "Same difference."

"Big difference."

Her gaze dropped to their hands. He did the same. Her hand looked so delicate entwined with his larger, darker one.

"If you say so." Glancing up, she laughed nervously and pulled her hand from his. She lifted her water glass to her lips and took an unsteady sip.

"We were never strangers, Kasey. That's why that night happened. Say what you will, but if we hadn't connected, had the attraction not been there, you wouldn't have gone with me. I'm sorry about your mother." Desperately he wished he could take away the pain she'd felt, still felt. "But I'm glad you came into Calista Blue and sat down beside me."

Biting her lower lip, she nodded, although he wasn't sure which part of his comments she was agreeing with.

"Let me be a part of your life."

"A relationship between us would make things messy." The green shade of her eyes grew darker. "Eventually, we'd part ways and then what? We'll have to work together every day and that could be disastrous."

There was more than what she was saying. She clearly spoke with the voice of experience. What else had happened to make her so skittish?

"I'm not going to promise you things I'm not sure I can keep. Neither am I sure what will happen between us in the future," he admitted, "but I care about you."

Her eyes softened at his admission. "You have no idea how much I want to say yes."

Not nearly as much as he wanted her to say yes.

"How about we take things one day at a time and see where that leads us?" He stared deep into her eyes, not hiding how much he wanted her to say yes. "If you want to keep things low-key because of work, fine, I'm game. Just give us a chance."

The afternoon flew by, which was a good thing because Kasey had a difficult time concentrating on her patients. She couldn't recall ever being distracted from her work before Eric. Not even Randall had interfered with her job. Not until after all hell had broken loose at Skymont, at any rate.

Pushing her glasses up the bridge of her nose, Kasey glanced up from the junk mail she flipped through to clear off her desk.

"Busy?" Eric leaned against her doorjamb, looking sexier than any man had a right to.

Seeing him in her doorway was getting to be a habit. One she'd be lying if she didn't admit to liking.

Her heart kicked up a beat. No wonder she'd been distracted all afternoon. Eric wanted her. What woman wouldn't be distracted?

"Just finishing for the day." She waved the conference flyer.

They'd gone back to the office after he'd suggested

a low-key relationship. He'd promised to stop by her office before leaving for the day. Which explained why she'd lingered.

Trying to keep her eyes locked with his and not roaming over his broad shoulders, flat abs and narrow hips encased in his slacks, she waited for him to say more.

Unfortunately, her gaze wandered when he stepped into the office and closed the door.

So did her mind.

She'd kissed those lips. Clung to those shoulders as she'd cried.

He'd held her. Tight. For real. As if he cared.

All she had to do was say *yes* and he would be holding her again.

She wanted him to hold her.

She pushed against her glasses, swallowed the lump in her throat.

"Why do you wear those?"

Her clothes? Certainly they'd grown too tight, as if she should rip them off. Just as they'd ripped off each other's clothes on the night they'd made love.

"My glasses?"

He nodded.

The better to see you with.

What was wrong with her? Why couldn't she look at him without remembering how he'd felt deep inside her body, how his strong heartbeat had mesmerized her.

"Why do people usually wear glasses?" she asked, knocking back the desire swamping her. He moved closer, and she got a whiff of pure testosterone-laden Eric. The man should bottle that and make his fortune.

"They're prescription?" he asked.

"Yes." There, she'd said yes. Yes. Yes. *Yes.* Now, would he please hurry up and kiss her?

Instead, he studied her face. "You didn't have them on the night we met."

She'd accidentally left them in her car seat when they'd fogged over from tears. She'd taken them off to clean her runny mascara. As steamed up as her insides had felt, she was surprised her glasses weren't fogged over right this minute.

"I wear them for reading and at work. I'm legal to drive, but definitely things are clearer when I have them on." Wow, she sounded normal, not like every nerve ending strained toward him, wanting an individual stroke. *Yes.*

He continued his slow perusal. "You had your hair down that night, too."

She touched her tightly pulled-back hair. "Loose hair gets in the way during work. My stethoscope gets tangled."

Too much information. Flustered, she shuffled through the stack of mail, gave Bones a don't-look-at-me-that-way look, anything to give her a moment to pull herself together.

Eric reached across her desk and did the unthinkable. First, he pulled the pins out of her hair and then her clip. Her dark hair fell to her shoulders. She wanted to run her fingers through the tangled mess in hope of restoring some kind of order. But she didn't move, she was so mesmerized by the look in Eric's eyes.

Hot liquid desire burned in his gaze.

Hot liquid desire burned inside her, paralyzing her. She waited to see what he'd do next.

Not one to disappoint, he retrieved the glasses from her face. With great care, he folded and placed them on her desk. "Better."

Better? What was with the critique? And why wasn't he kissing her? She'd said yes. "If you don't like how I look, don't look."

"I do."

"You do what?" She moistened her dry lips.

"Like how you look." Eric pulled her to her feet. With exaggerated slowness he grazed his fingertips over the smoothness of her cheek, along her jaw, then brushed over her slightly parted mouth.

"You are beautiful, but you try to disguise that beauty with those." He gestured to the glasses on her desk. "And those." He nodded at the hair clips. "It doesn't work, Kasey. Your beauty shines through."

She snorted. "That's why men are beating down my door."

"Well," he agreed with a crooked smile, "I didn't exactly beat down your door, but I do show up here quite often."

His fingers slipped into her hair, cupped the base of her head, massaged her scalp.

Heat blazed in her cheeks, in her chest, lower.

He bent his head, pausing within centimeters of her lips. Staring into her eyes, he waited, his hot breath moist and tempting.

She knew what he wanted, what he waited for.

She closed the distance between them, pressing her lips to his, taking what she'd wanted for what seemed like forever.

Tension she hadn't been aware he'd been giving off eased. Tension she hadn't noticed because her own had been so overpowering.

He might have let her take the initiative, might have given her the opportunity to stop him had his kiss not been what she wanted. But he took her kiss as the key to open the floodgates of chemistry between them.

With every brush of his lips over hers, every thrust of his tongue into her mouth, Eric stole bits of her soul.

"Kasey," he breathed into her mouth, his hands roving over her neck, her shoulders, her back. "I've wanted to kiss you like this for so long."

Weren't they her thoughts exactly?

His mouth covered hers again.

Kasey forgot where she was, why she was, who she was. All she knew was Eric. Eric's mouth, his lips, his tongue, his minty taste. Had he brushed his teeth or eaten a mint? Had he known he would kiss her? Had they really come that far with just one lunch date where he'd asked her to give him a chance?

If they hadn't come that far, why wasn't she lambasting him instead of kissing him back?

Because this was what she wanted. To touch him, kiss him, feel his long, hard body pressed to hers.

Dear sweet heaven above, he was hard.

With another lingering kiss he pulled back. "I have to stop before I forget where we are and we do something we shouldn't. Before I take you right here, right now, because I'm damned tempted."

He glanced meaningfully at her desk and a vivid vision of the two of them, naked, tangled together on her desk, popped into Kasey's mind, blending with the emotional flood she was already drowning in.

She blinked, awed by the magic that he'd wielded with the sweep of his tongue into her mouth. How had he done that?

Sure, she had memories of their previous kisses, but she'd been devastated, drinking that delicious fruity concoction he'd ordered for her. She'd been sure her imagination played tricks on her recall of those kisses.

Her memory hadn't done him justice.

The man could kiss. And how.

"Kasey?" Eric tilted her head toward him and stared into her glazed eyes. "Say something, sweetheart. Tell me you aren't going cold on me."

"Cold on you?" She pulled free of his embrace and scooted back, almost knocking the framed diploma from her wall. Her movements were jerky, evidence that he wasn't the only one shaken by what they'd shared. "Cold is the last thing a woman could feel after kisses like those."

She covered her mouth with her hand, her wide eyes staring at him in disbelief at what she'd said.

He grinned. Damn, she was cute. And extremely kissable. He'd like to kiss her some more. Lots more.

"Does that mean you're ready to go to dinner? Or that you'd like to forgo food altogether?"

"I..." She paused, inhaled deeply, shook when he took her hands into his. "We agreed to tread lightly until we know this isn't a mistake."

He heard her words, but it was the pain in her eyes that spoke the loudest. "What's his name?"

"Who?" She didn't look away, but her eyes became shielded all the same.

"The man who made you so afraid of relationships."

"What makes you ask that?" She blinked.

"It's obvious some guy did a number on you and now you've closed yourself off from the world." Even as he said the words out loud, he recognized their truth. "That's why you hide behind your glasses. You don't want to be noticed, do you? Not as a desirable woman, at any rate. Being ignored is much safer. Keeping me at arm's length is safer than admitting you enjoyed making love with me."

She jerked her hands free. "You have no right to say those things to me."

"But I'm right, aren't I?" he pushed. "I may have only been here a few weeks, but I suspect I know you better than anyone who works at the clinic."

"You are so arrogant," she accused.

"Tell me I'm wrong."

"You're wrong," she immediately spat at him.

"And you're a liar."

Her mouth fell open, and she gawked at him. "How dare you say that to me?"

"You'll find I dare a lot of things," he promised, tweaking her nose. "It's time someone started making you face the truth, made you start living life again. Part of living is taking chances."

He was probably the last person who should offer advice on living life. Hell, he'd run from his life, spent as much time away from Rivendell as possible. Years. Perhaps it took one to know one, but Kasey had only been scratching the surface of who she was. A simple life helping others, finding the person beneath his heritage had made Eric realize who he was, who he wanted to be. He wasn't so sure Kasey really knew the beautiful woman who stared back at her from the mirror.

If nothing else came from them having met, he hoped he could help her see the wonderful, strong woman he saw.

"I have a good life."

He cupped her face, caressing her cheek with his thumb. "Which is why you came in search of a stranger on the night of your mother's funeral."

Whatever Kasey thought of Eric's comment, she'd only grabbed her purse and asked where they were going to dinner.

Eric opted not to take her to any of the restaurants where they might run into someone who knew them. Instead, he drove into Lexington. They ate at an Italian restaurant he hadn't visited since returning to the States.

"This is really good," Kasey mused, taking a bite of a bread stick not long from the oven.

"It used to be one of my favorites."

"Used to be?"

"I spent four years in Africa."

"I'd heard something along those lines when you first started." She smiled. "The rumor mill is well and alive at the Rivendell Medical Center. What exactly did you do in Africa? I always thought working overseas would be fascinating."

"Working overseas is fascinating." He told her about

some of his jobs while there. "Of course, there were a few occasions where it was a little too fascinating."

"Oh?"

"I worked in Darfur for a while."

Kasey's face paled. "But isn't there a war there?"

Eric shrugged. "The poor of war-torn countries tend to be those who need medical care the most."

Dropping the remainder of her bread stick onto her plate, Kasey eyed him suspiciously. "Are you really as great as you seem?"

He grinned. "I'm better, but you already know that."

Smiling, she rolled her eyes. But she didn't deny his claim.

He told her about the months he'd spent working in a Sudanese medical camp, the months he'd spent in a Ethiopian medical convoy, about his favorite memories of the time he'd spent overseas.

"I've never traveled outside the U.S., but hope to some day."

"What's keeping you from doing so now?"

A puzzled look came over her face. "I'm not sure," she admitted. "I tend to work long hours."

"Unless you really mismanaged your practice contract, you should have generous vacation time," he pointed out.

"I do, but somehow I end up at the clinic even when I'm scheduled off."

"That's no fun."

"No." She shook her head, looking surprised at her admission. "It isn't."

Later that night, she gave him her home phone number. He already had her cell-phone number from the clinic.

Standing in the vacant Rivendell Medical Center parking lot where they'd left her car, he kissed her goodnight, then watched her drive away.

He hadn't pressed for more. He suspected if he'd pressed she wouldn't have turned him away. He also suspected that if they made love before she trusted him, he'd never have her trust.

He wanted Kasey's trust.

Later that night he lay in his bed, phone pressed to his ear, and swapped medical school stories with a woman who would someday trust him.

A trust he'd work hard to earn and do his best never to lose.

Two weeks later, at the ambulatory clinic, Kasey saw a diabetic who'd stepped on a sharp rock while outside barefoot despite her distinctly recalling discussing that diabetics should never go barefoot, particularly outdoors.

Next, she performed a gynecological exam on a young woman who was having pelvic pain. As the woman's cytology exam hadn't been performed in over a year, she ran the liquid preparation and made three microscope slides to do an in-house vaginal survey.

Kasey applied the appropriate solution to each slide, placed them inside a transport container, then headed to the clinic's small lab to do the gram stain. They could do simple laboratory tests in-house, like a urinalysis, glucose, rapid Strep, pregnancy and a vaginal survey, without having to send to Rivendell's main laboratory.

"Hey, you. I've not seen you today," Eric said, stepping into the lab. "Need any help?"

Kasey's breath caught in her throat. Her heart leaped with joy as it seemed to always do when he was near.

Since the night he'd driven them to the Italian restaurant in Lexington, they'd either dined together or met after she worked on the masquerade ball.

Each night ended the same surprising way. With Eric kissing her goodnight. Admittedly, hot and heavy kissing, but she'd expected him to push for a repeat performance of the night they'd met.

He hadn't.

They spent their time talking, laughing, getting to know each other. Which threw her. If he only wanted a physical relationship with her, why invest the time to get to know her?

"I've still got a few patients to see, if that's what you're asking."

"Me, too."

No matter how much she tried to focus on what she was doing, she couldn't. She glanced up, found her lips lifting into a smile.

"Then perhaps you should finish with yours, instead of watching me," she suggested. She couldn't help but smile. Not when he was looking at her like she was the lollipop that was going to send him into a diabetic coma and he'd die a happy man. She took a step back, knowing that if he kissed her, she'd be a goner. Work was no place for such shenanigans.

Grinning, he stepped closer. "Rough day?"

"I've been swamped." And she had a meeting with

the Rivendell Ladies Society fund-raiser committee tonight. A meeting she wasn't looking forward to since Gladys Anderson had yet to return her calls regarding publicity for the event. "Haven't you?"

"Steady stream of gastrointestinal disturbances," he told her. "Not my favorite thing to treat."

"You have a favorite?"

"Yes, but we'd have to discuss that in private." He waggled his eyebrows.

She rolled her eyes.

"Have dinner plans tonight, Kasey?"

"I do." She'd hoped to have time to go home, shower, look her best before heading to the fancy restaurant where the RLS met. She'd be lucky if she had time to apply a fresh coat of lipstick.

"Lucky bastard." Eric grinned smugly. "Anyone I know?"

"I don't think so."

His grin faltered. "You weren't referring to dinner with me?"

"No. I really do have plans."

His face an unreadable mask, he considered her a moment. "With a man?"

"With a group of ladies I volunteer with. I'm on the fund-raiser committee. We're meeting to discuss progress and to make sure everything is set."

He relaxed a little, toying with a strand of her hair he'd worked loose from her clip. "Sounds exciting."

Did it? Being on a committee, helping plan activities, that had been her dream for so long. Now she was a fully fledged junior member on her way to becoming a fully fledged member of the RLS. She was rising above her background, becoming somebody. Lord, she was even dating the most gorgeous man in Rivendell.

She lifted her chin with pride. "It's for a good cause."

His eyes glittering with a mischievous gleam, he arched one brow. "Dinner with me isn't?"

"I suspect dinner with you would cause more bad than good."

"Don't you believe it," he warned, taking another step toward her, their bodies almost touching from where he stood beside her. This playfulness reminded her of how they'd talked at the bar. They'd sat in that booth for hours, talking, flirting, enjoying each other's company.

Wanting to put a halt to his advance, she glanced at the slide she'd placed under the microscope clips. Hmm. Had that been a sperm or a parasite she'd seen wiggle its tail? She hadn't gotten a good look, but she suspected a parasite based upon the woman's symptoms.

Kasey used the knobs on the microscope to move the slide so she could get a better view. There. Definitely a parasite. And the patient's other symptoms and her history fit the diagnosis.

"See something interesting?"

"Yes," she answered, glancing up from examining the slide to let her gaze slide over him.

"May I?" He leaned beside her to peer into the microscope eyepiece. "Fascinating little creatures, aren't they?"

Fascinating? She could think of a few other descriptive terms she'd apply.

"Do you see a lot of sexually transmitted diseases at the clinic?" he asked, straightening up but not moving away from how close he stood. His body heat practically enveloped her.

"Most go to the gynecologist, but a fair amount do see us. Particularly if they aren't sure what's going on. Or if they're seen through the charity fund."

"I thought those being seen through the charity could go to the specialists, too."

"They can if we refer them. We're the starting point for all care provided through the charity. Which is why it's important I go to my meeting tonight. Without funds being raised, the charity wouldn't be able to provide care to the working poor of this community."

Disappointment lit his eyes, but he nodded. "Okay."

"I can't have dinner with you, but I would like to see you tonight."

"We could get together after you finish," he suggested, obviously surprised by her admission. "We could meet for coffee."

Kasey smiled. "That sounds perfect. After my meeting I'll likely need someone to vent to."

"Oh?" His brow quirked. "Are you having problems?"

Kasey sighed, wondering if she'd imagined Doreen Von Buren's hostility at the last meeting. "Nothing I can't handle."

That evening, Kasey sat at the table with half a dozen longtime Rivendell Ladies Society matrons. What was it she'd been thinking earlier about rising above her upbringing?

With a single haughty look from Doreen Von Buren she'd been reduced to feelings of incompetence.

She tapped her pen against her notebook and stared at the list of things she needed to accomplish prior to the charity fund-raiser for the clinic. She was competent, capable, their equal in every way. She'd do such a great job on this fund-raiser that they'd beg her to be a member of their group.

"Have you spoken with the *Rivendell Gazette* yet?" asked the petite platinum blonde, who constantly looked as if she wore a too-tight ponytail, even when she wore her hair loose.

Doreen Von Buren.

If not for the fact the woman had a daughter in her early twenties, Kasey wouldn't begin to be able to guess her age. Her skin was flawless. Doreen dressed immaculately, attended all the right social functions, knew all the right people. Doreen was exactly what Kasey had dreamed of as a child, what she'd aspired to someday become. A wealthy, respected member of society who gave back to the community and made the world a better place by being in it.

Someone who was the opposite of Betsy.

"I bumped into Gladys Anderson of the Lifestyles section," Doreen continued. "She mentioned she hadn't heard from you. We're less than a month out. Don't you think you're cutting the press too close?"

"The initial press release has run." Needlessly, Kasey scribbled down the all-too-familiar name on her list. She'd meticulously kept notes of even the tiniest detail in regard to the masquerade ball. "I've left messages a couple of times about Gladys doing a feature on the event. She hasn't called me back. I faxed another news release to the main editor and plan to do so again this week."

"Oh, dear." Doreen inflected her voice with great concern. "She probably doesn't recognize your name and has just been busy. She did do that wonderful write-up on my daughter last week."

Gladys was an RLS member wannabe, just like Kasey. Until this year Kasey had merely been a lackey, someone to take tickets at the front door, someone to set up the chairs, someone to go door-to-door collecting donations. Not this year. This year she'd been asked to serve as a junior member on the fund-raiser committee. A big step in the right direction and perhaps one that had caused a bit of jealousy.

A commotion at the entrance of the restaurant caused all six women to turn. Ella, Doreen's daughter, who Gladys had apparently gone on and on about in the social section, entered the restaurant. Late as usual, she paused dramatically for everyone to bask in her pale blond glow.

Kasey was struck with a mixture of admiration and jealousy. Admiration of the way Ella accepted the world as her due, how she belonged no matter where she went, at how she oozed class and sophistication. She'd bet her eyeteeth Ella had never gone to bed hungry, that she'd never hidden in a closet to escape one of her mother's drunken rages, that she'd never shopped at garage sales for clothes with money she'd made from doing odd jobs for neighbors, or worn long sleeves in the dead of summer to hide bruises.

Ella lived the life Kasey had grown up dreaming of to escape the reality of her own sad life. Ella looked like High Society Barbie. All she needed to complete the look was a tall, dark and handsome man. Eric popped into Kasey's mind. Eric and Ella would make a beautiful couple. Actually, Ella was exactly the kind of woman Kasey imagined Eric would someday end up married to. Young, beautiful, sophisticated, well bred.

But Ella couldn't have Eric. Kasey reached up to touch her temple, but resisted the urge to massage the pounding there. No, Ella couldn't have Eric because for the moment he belonged to *her*.

For two weeks he'd treated her like the queen of the world. His world, at any rate.

Just as soon as this meeting was finished, she'd meet him for coffee. Right then and there she promised herself that she'd give him a huge hug for the joy he'd added to her life.

Sure, she worried about his meetings with Mr. Evans and some of the older board members, but her life had become Technicolor the moment she'd agreed to let Eric be a part of it.

On Sunday afternoon he'd even convinced her to get on a horse. Her. On a horse. She hadn't even fallen off. Then again, Eric had been on the horse, too. All she'd had to do was keep her arms wrapped around his waist while they'd ridden over the lush Kentucky hills to where he'd arranged a picnic lunch.

The memory put a smile back onto Kasey's face.

Ella air-kissed her mother's cheeks. "Tell me what I've missed."

"Only that Kasey hasn't been able to get in touch with Gladys from the *Gazette*."

Ugh. There went her smile again.

"No problem," Ella assured her before Kasey could speak, sliding into the vacant chair and shaking out a white napkin into her lap. Their waiter miraculously appeared, placed a water glass and a glass of white wine in front of her, earning himself a gracious smile from the platinum blonde. "I'll call Gladys in the morning. What do we need? A feature story on the masquerade ball and a couple of well-placed advertisements?"

"I don't mind calling her again," Kasey said, hating the wave of incompetence washing over her. She'd visit the paper during her lunch break if that's what she had to do to get the issue cleared.

"There's no need," Doreen cut in, her tone brisk, condemning. "My daughter will see that our publicity gets done. Some have a natural talent for these things. Some don't."

Kasey felt the sting of the reprimand.

"Fine." She smiled brightly at Ella. "That'll give me more time to work with the caterer."

"The caterer?" Reva Talley asked from her seat at the table. Again, her age was fairly undeterminable and her plastic surgeon likely a wealthy man. Reva might be forty. She might be sixty.

"I've hired Dellarosa's."

"Didn't we have problems with them?" Doreen's nose curled. "You should have gone with the one we used last year."

"They were already booked," Kasey reminded her,

knowing she'd already gone over this with the committee months ago. She'd gone with Dellarosa's at their emphatic recommendation.

"Then perhaps you should act sooner next year instead of waiting until the last minute. If you're even asked to serve."

Kasey blinked at the woman in confusion. Where had that come from?

"Now, Mother." Ella patted her mother's bony arm sympathetically. "You must remember Kasey is new to this. After all, she isn't really an RLS member."

Outwardly, Kasey cast a fake smile of gratitude. Inwardly, she winced.

Just when she was starting to feel like her life was coming together professionally, personally and socially, people like the Von Burens brought her crashing back down to reality.

Not that she didn't sometimes feel like there was a drastic social chasm between Eric and herself. Not that he ever came across as a snob, he didn't. No, he just did things like calmly announce that the elaborate horse farm they'd visited belonged to his family. No big deal. And because he'd truly acted as if it weren't a big deal, Kasey had eventually relaxed.

Perhaps his years of simple living in Africa had stamped out whatever elitism he might have once had.

That's what she told herself, at any rate.

That a man who would spend four years in third-world countries when he could be sitting at home in the lap of luxury wasn't the kind of man to care if she'd been born with a silver spoon in her mouth or a copy of the *Trailer Park Gazette* in her hands.

Most of the time she convinced herself. Because it was what she desperately wanted to believe.

A week later, Eric smiled at the young woman sitting on the exam table. She couldn't be more than twenty-five. Three small children buzzed around the room with more energy than any one person should have to cope with and a year-old baby squirmed in her lap. Three girls and a boy who looked to be the oldest and was oblivious to all the commotion his sisters were causing. He played with two toy cars in the floor and was lost in his pretend world of play.

"What brings you into the clinic?" he asked, smiling as the toddler dug her fingers into her mother's shirt, clinging tightly to the material while she eyed him suspiciously. Her big, almost black eyes followed his every movement and she didn't return his smile.

"I need a refill on my thyroid medicine." Belinda Peters pried the little fingers loose from her shirt and shifted the wiggling little girl on her lap.

Eric glanced down at the medical record. Sure enough, she was on a thyroid tablet and an antidepressant.

"No problem. I'll write the prescription and a lab slip for you to have your thyroid levels checked." His gaze continued to skim over her record. Her other medication usually needed to be renewed at the same time. "What about your antidepressant? Do you need a refill on that, too?"

"Jackie! Get down from there," she called to the

little girl who looked to be about three and was attempting to climb onto the table that housed numerous medical supplies.

Jackie shot her mother an assessing look, decided tempting fate was safe, and kept right on climbing.

With an exasperated sigh, Belinda jumped from the exam table, sat her youngest in the floor and scooped Jackie into her arms. "Sit here, and be good."

The little girl didn't seem happy with her mother's interference. Actually, she seemed downright upset as she twisted and arched in her mother's grasp. "Let go," she howled over and over. The baby on the floor glanced from Eric to her screaming sister to her mother. Her lower lip trembled and big tears welled in her eyes. The third little girl eyed her brother's toy cars, a mischievous gleam in her eyes.

First waylaying the baby's tears with a squeaky toy, Belinda dug in the diaper bag, produced another toy car, which she handed to her other daughter, wrapped her arms protectively around Jackie, then smiled weakly at Eric.

"Sorry. You were saying?"

No wonder the poor woman looked exhausted.

He'd never thought much about kids, although certainly his mother had been hinting enough that it was past time he produced a grandchild for her to spoil. Hinting? More like she'd been parading a constant bevy of possible daughter-in-law candidates. All upper-crust young beauties who were mainly the spoilt daughters of her various well-to-do acquaintances.

Now that he felt comfortable Kasey wasn't using him, he needed to tell his mother about her. Last night, when his mother had questioned him about who was taking up so much of his time, he'd been evasive, not wanting her interference where Kasey was concerned. Not at this stage in their relationship.

His mother could be forceful if you didn't know how to deal with her. Forceful being a bulldozer until she wore you down. She'd learned long ago those tactics didn't work on Eric, but the rest of the world was fair game.

"I was asking about your antidepressant. Do you need a refill of that one, too?"

Squeaking the baby's discarded toy duck and placing it in the baby's hands, Belinda made a quacking noise as she shook her head. "I'm not taking it anymore. Quack. Quack."

"Did Dr. Carmichael discontinue it?" The chart didn't show Kasey having done so, and she documented meticulously. When he saw one of her patients, all the pertinent details were usually right in her notes.

Jackie continued to squirm in her mother's lap, but Belinda kept a firm grip on her daughter while she eyed her two-year-old who, bored with the toy car, contemplated the table her sister had wanted to scale. The baby had stuck the squeaky toy in her mouth and was currently content to gnaw on the head of the rubber duck. "Quack."

"That's right, baby girl. Quack. Quack. I took myself off," the young mother admitted, only half her attention on Eric. "Sara, come over here. Now."

He smiled at the middle child, who apparently wanted to mimic her big sister's every move, and won himself a toothy grin in response. Taking out a couple of tongue depressors, he lifted the child into his lap and handed them to her. Before the little girl got bored with the sticks, Eric turned back to his patient. "Why? Are you feeling better?"

Not wanting to be ignored, Sara wiped a wet stick across his hand. He glanced at the slobber on his fingers, at the little girl in his lap. Unable to resist the mixture of innocence and mischief, Eric smiled. Sara rewarded him with a sloppy kiss on his cheek. "Quack. Quack," she announced merrily.

Eric's heart melted. He'd taken care of kids in the past, thousands while working in Africa. But he didn't recall having one plant a kiss on him. The oddly nice feeling made him wonder if he shouldn't rethink his no-kids thing.

Just like that, an image of him and Kasey making a baby shot into his head, closely followed by the image of a little girl with Kasey's gorgeous green eyes and his dimples popping a kiss on him, melting his heart, wrapping him around her little finger.

Never had he visualized having a child, but the image in his mind was so vivid his heart ached at the knowledge she didn't exist.

Eric reeled, almost to the point he forgot to breathe.

To the point he almost missed what Belinda Peters was saying.

"I didn't like being on another medication, and I didn't like the side effects." Belinda's arms remained securely around her daughter. Jackie twisted and turned in her mother's arms to no avail. "So I quit taking it."

Clearing his head of his unexpected paternal longing, Eric forced himself to focus on his patient. "Can you feel a difference since you've come off the medicine?"

The woman's eyes cut to the two kids on the floor. The squeaky toy held the baby's attention, and the four-year-old little boy pushed the toy car Sara hadn't wanted along the floor, making engine noises and unaware of his mother's watchful eye.

"I cry a lot and don't sleep as well, but I didn't like feeling medicated. It's an okay trade-off. I get by. I saw on the news where this woman was taking the same antidepressant I was on. She lost her mind and hurt her kids." She described the incident in question. "Thoughts like those are the last thing I need at this point in my life."

With Sara content in his lap, Eric spent the next ten minutes discussing the pros and cons of antidepressants. Should he suggest she restart on a different medication that hopefully wouldn't cause side effects? Two minutes more and he knew he should. Still, if he didn't hurry along he'd be behind for the rest of the afternoon and wouldn't be able to see his share of the drop-in patients.

Which meant Kasey would have to pick up the slack. Thinking of Kasey caused his earlier vision to flash through his head again before he could stop the disturbing image.

As unexpected as it had been, the image of him and Kasey having a child together had been…nice.

Which scared the hell out of him.

Maybe he just needed sex. Hell, he did need sex. With Kasey. Badly. But until she said she was ready, he'd restrain himself. On Sunday he'd wanted to push her back onto the blanket they'd picnicked on and make love to her. He hadn't, but he'd wanted to.

After finishing his discussion with the young mother,

Eric went to set Sara down. She surprised him by wrapping her arms around his neck, clinging tightly and shaking her head.

"Hey, sweetheart," he said in soft voice. "It's time for you to go home."

"No." The little girl clung tighter and began showering him with more wet kisses.

"Sara, don't do that," her mother ordered, handing her son the diaper bag into which they'd placed the toys. She picked up the baby and grabbed hold of Jackie's hand. Just in the nick of time as Jackie had made a beeline toward the cabinet. "She's getting you all wet. I can take her."

How? he wondered. Her hands were already full. He wasn't sure what type of support Belinda had, but he planned to find out, see if he couldn't get her into a parenting class or support group to make her life easier.

"No problem. I'll help you get this sweetie pie to the car." He stepped into the hallway and immediately bumped into the object of his thoughts. The constant object of his thoughts.

Kasey smiled. Eric's heart sang.

"Hi." He beamed, amazed at how her smile brightened the place like a beam of sunshine.

Her gaze dropped to the toddler in his arms, then back up to stare. Her eyes held an awed wonder. As if the image of him holding the little girl caused baby visions in Kasey's head, too.

Now, that really should scare him.

The last thing he needed was Kasey or any woman getting baby thoughts involving him.

"Can you say hello to Dr. Carmichael?" he said to the

toddler, who continued to coat his cheeks with two-year-old high gloss.

"What's your name, sweetheart?" Kasey asked in the softest, kindest voice he'd ever heard.

"This is Sara."

"That's a beautiful name," Kasey said. "Would you like a sticker?"

"Me. Me. I want a sticker," Jackie piped up from where her mother held her hand in a tight grip. Her free hand waved wildly through the air.

"Me, too," the quiet little boy said.

Sara nodded, suddenly acting shy and burying her face into Eric's shirt.

"Here, Dr. Carmichael, I think these are just what the doctor ordered." Lora handed Kasey a handful of stickers to distribute then left to call another patient.

The little boy tugged on his shirt, indicating a spot for Kasey to put a sticker. She applied an airplane one and handed him a few others to attach wherever he saw fit. She stuck a funny-faced bumblebee sticker to Jackie's shirt. The girl clapped in glee and burst into a rendition of "Bringing home a baby bumblebee, won't my momma be so proud of me".

Kasey put a bright red flower sticker on Sara's shirt. "There. You look gorgeous." She bent forward and pretended to smell the blossom. "And don't you just smell sweet as a rose?"

Sara giggled.

Laughing softly, Kasey's gaze met Eric's and a mischievous gleam lit her eyes. "I think Dr. Matthews deserves a sticker, too. What do you think?"

Sara nodded and Jackie clapped again, beginning another round of her song while she danced around in hyper circles.

Kasey flipped through the remaining stickers, smiling when she found the one she wanted. A big, puffy "SUPER." Peeling the protective backing off, she pressed it right above his heart. Her fingers lingered, smoothing the surrounding material. "Perfect."

Did she feel how his heart galloped as if he ran the Kentucky Derby? At the rate he was going he'd win the roses.

Belinda turned to him. "Thank you, Dr. Matthews. I'll take Sara from here."

Eric offered to help them to the car, but Belinda seemed to have everything under control as Jackie led her siblings in another verse about the bumblebee.

When the family had gone, Eric met Kasey's gaze and waggled his brows. "You think I'm super?"

Smile in place, she dramatically rolled her eyes. "It was either that or a fuzzy white bunny who said 'Have a hoppy day'," she fibbed, heading back toward her office.

"Right." Following her, he pointedly looked at the stickers still in her hands. "Hoppy has some company there."

Kasey laughed and stuck them in her lab-coat pocket. "Okay, you got me."

The moment they were inside her office and the door was closed, he leaned toward her, breathing in her sweet scent. "So, answer my question. Do you think I'm super?"

She put her finger to the side of her mouth and pretended to give his question some thought. "Can you leap tall buildings?"

"No." Eric took her into his arms.

"Are you faster than a speeding bullet?"

"No." He pulled her to him.

"Stronger than a locomotive?"

"Depends on what you mean by strong." He shifted his body against hers.

Kasey ignored his blatantly suggestive gesture. "Hmm, you're not doing too well on the superhero quiz."

"Maybe you should ask me better questions," he recommended, nuzzling her neck.

"Do you have a cape and wear your underwear on the outside of a pair of tights?"

Eric laughed. "Not since I was five."

She sighed in exaggerated disappointment, simultaneously arching her neck to give him better access. His tongue traced over the delicate skin, laving her earlobe in a caress.

"There's only one superhero test left," she said a bit breathily. "If you fail, I'm afraid it's hoppy time for you."

"Uh-oh." He sucked her earlobe into his mouth, giving the tender flesh a gentle nip. "This sounds serious."

"Very." Her hands moved to his shoulders. She splayed her fingers, holding tightly to him. "Do you have any fatal weaknesses? You know, like kryptonite?"

"Nope, but I'm hard as a rock," he admitted, shifting his hips against hers to prove his point. "Does that count?"

Pink tinged Kasey's face. "Uh, no, but I'm pretty sure that…" she moved against him "…is automatic qualification for super status."

Eric kissed her mouth, fully and freely, just as he'd kissed her every day for the past three weeks. And as with each of those times, kissing Kasey left him wanting more.

"Maybe I do have a fatal weakness." He paused for effect. "Kaseynite."

Her smile slipped. "I make you feel weak?"

Maybe his attempt to be cute hadn't come out right.

"That's not what I meant," he told her, wrapping his arms around her waist and holding her to him. He stared into her eyes and hoped she saw the truth. "Especially since you make me feel like I could leap those tall buildings and run faster than a speeding bullet."

As he'd hoped, Kasey smiled.

She stretched onto tiptoes and kissed his cheek. "Nice save, my superhero."

CHAPTER SIX

THE clinic was swamped with gastrointestinal disorders. Some real. Some imagined. A bad shipment of tomatoes had hit the supermarkets and the media was having a sensationalist field day with it as nothing else newsworthy was going on.

Over the past few days, the number of cases had slowed, but the clinic remained busy. So did Kasey. With preparations for the fund-raiser and with Eric.

She worried about what she saw as their inevitable breakup, but she wasn't a coward. She'd take each day, enjoy her time with him and deal with whatever the future held.

"Dr. Carmichael?" Lora poked her head into the exam room where Kasey was finishing entering prescriptions for a forty-five-year-old's seizure medications. "Sorry to interrupt, but I just put an acute abdomen in room four."

Another food poisoning?

"I'll be right there." Kasey smiled at the epileptic patient, handed him his billing sheet and followed Lora. "What's going on?"

"Mr. Oliver is in room four."

"With abdominal pain?" Poor Mr. Oliver. She hoped he hadn't gotten the stomach bug.

Lora nodded. "Dr. Matthews is in with him, but he asked to see you. Dr. Matthews told me to get you."

Dr. Matthews. Eric. Kasey's heart flip-flopped in her chest.

"Thanks," Kasey told Lora.

She knocked on the door, pasted a smile on her face and entered the exam room. Kasey's gaze touched on Eric, her heart beating faster as it always did when she saw him, before turning her full attention to the older gentleman lying on the exam table. "Hi, Mr. Oliver, what's going on?"

"That's what I'm here to find out from you." He winced every time Eric pressed on his abdomen.

"When did your stomach start hurting? You were in the office a few weeks ago about your lower back. Was your stomach hurting then?"

"Not really." He didn't sound convincing.

"Not really? What does that mean?"

"It means it was bothering me, but not bad enough to mention."

"When did it get bad enough to bring you in? This morning?"

"I got to hurting last night. Threw up several times. Nasty bile-looking stuff. Thought I was going to have to go to the emergency room. I took extra of my back medicine. The pain eased up enough to hold off. This morning I tried going to work, but the vomiting started again. Joe drove me here." He placed his hands over his abdomen in response to Eric's palpations. "That hurts."

"Right there?" Eric asked, pressing over the man's upper right quadrant.

Mr. Oliver nodded. "Like a knife is cutting into me straight through to my shoulder blade."

Eric pressed deeper, pushing his fingertips slightly up under the edge of Mr. Oliver's rib cage. The man's breath caught.

"Hard to breathe when you touch me there," he gasped.

Eric and Kasey exchanged looks. A positive Murphy's sign.

"Have you ever had any abdominal surgeries, Mr. Oliver? Specifically, do you have your gallbladder?"

"I have everything God gave me," the man claimed between winces. "Can you fix me, Doc?" His gaze went back and forth between Kasey and Eric. "'Cause I can't work like this and I can't afford not to work. Family has got to eat."

"You need an ultrasound of your gallbladder, Mr. Oliver. While Dr. Matthews continues to examine you, I'm going to call radiology and see if they can squeeze you in this afternoon."

"Is he okay?" Lora asked when Kasey stepped into the hallway. Mr. Oliver was one of those patients the entire clinic adored. Probably because he worked so hard to take care of his family and his love for them always shone through.

"Who?" Jonathan asked, coming out of a patient room. His skin glowed from his vacation. His gaze settled on Lora and lingered.

Interesting.

"An acute abdomen who came in earlier," Lora said, her cheeks glowing but not from the sun.

Not acknowledging Lora's blush or her explanation, Jonathan averted his gaze to Kasey and smiled. "We've had too many abdominal issues lately."

His friendly tone surprised Kasey. He had never paid her much attention. Why would he now?

Unless he and Eric had been talking again. Unless Jonathan knew who Eric had been spending his evenings with, sometimes until near midnight.

"I need to call Radiology," she said, and walked away. When they'd agreed to keep their relationship quiet, had Eric included his best friend in that agreement?

Did it matter if he hadn't?

"Kase?" Jonathan came into her office just as she finished getting the okay for sending Mr. Oliver for the needed test. "Can I talk to you a minute?"

"About?"

"Eric."

"Why would you want to discuss Dr. Matthews with me?"

"Look, I made some comments I shouldn't have on the day I introduced you two." He had the grace to look ashamed. "I owe you an apology."

"Weeks have gone by. Why would you apologize now?"

"You're seeing him, aren't you?"

"I see him every day. At work."

"You know what I'm saying." His gaze narrowed and an apologetic expression morphed into an accusatory one. "The thing is, you've made no secret that you want a spot on the medical board and you belong to that women's club. You can't blame me for wondering if you have ulterior motives where Eric's concerned."

Ulterior motives? What was he talking about? No, she wasn't going to ask. Gut instincts she'd learned to listen to long ago told her not to discuss Eric, that, despite his apology, Eric's friend was who had ulterior motives.

"I'll be honest. I'm still not a hundred percent convinced you're for real. I know about Skymont." He dropped his bombshell. "That you'd do anything to move up the career ladder. Despite the easygoing man you see, Eric has had his share of problems. I don't want to see him get hurt."

Kasey reeled. She hadn't known anyone at Rivendell knew what had happened at Skymont. Hadn't she once worried that becoming involved with Eric would somehow dredge up her past? Had Dr. Douglas become worried about the woman his friend was seeing and hired an investigator to dig up the skeletons in her closet? What else had he found?

"Dr. Douglas." She kept her tone crisp, but polite. "I don't think we should discuss my relationship with Dr. Matthews."

"Perhaps not, but he cares about you. I care about him. He's a good guy. Don't hurt him."

Eric's best friend leaned against the cabinet Bones stood on. Both wore staunch expressions.

"Jonathan?" Eric said, stepping into the room but not making it further than the entrance due to the room's size. Immediately sensing the hostility, he looked back and forth between them. "What's going on?"

Dr. Douglas shook his head. "Just checking on the acute abdomen."

Eric's forehead wrinkled. "You know Mr. Oliver?"

"He's seen members of the Oliver family," Kasey interrupted, watching as Dr. Douglas stepped out of her office.

After one last look at his friend, Eric met her gaze in question.

"Radiology says to send Mr. Oliver now."

Standing in his office, Eric peered over Kasey's shoulder as she read Mr. Oliver's radiology report on the computer screen. The last of the patients had been seen for the day and she'd stopped by his recently finished office to see if he'd heard anything.

"Acute cholethiasis."

He'd just read the report a few minutes prior to her knock.

"It's what we suspected," Eric said, watching Kasey study the monitor. "I've called the surgeon, but apparently the only one working through the charity is on vacation for two weeks. Dr. Willis is covering for him, but isn't willing to rearrange his schedule for a patient he won't make anything on."

"Dr. Willis?" Kasey curled her nose. "He wouldn't be my first choice, anyway, but I suppose we have no choice. So, when is he willing to work in Mr. Oliver?"

"Next Monday."

Kasey grimaced. "A week from now? We can't let Mr. Oliver suffer that long. Even if we heavily medicate him to ease the pain, he'll end up dehydrated or worse. Plus, he'll keep trying to work."

"I agree."

She stood, paced across his office. "I'll call one of the other surgeons. See if I can convince one of them to agree to do the surgery."

"Or I could do the surgery," he suggested, watching her face for her reaction. In a large facility like Rivendell Medical Center where specialists abounded, doctors working in ambulatory care didn't ordinarily perform surgical procedures.

Green eyes widened. "You?"

"Don't look so shocked," he teased. "I'm trained. When I was working overseas, I never knew what was going to walk into my tent. I've done a little of everything. A gallbladder removal in a state-of-the-art surgi-center really isn't that big a deal."

"You'd do his surgery?" She sounded incredulous. "Here, at the surgi-center?"

"If you'll go in with me."

Her brows knitted into a vee. "You might be a trained surgeon, but I'm not. I've never performed anything as extensive as a gallbladder removal."

"I'd like you to be there with me. Will you?"

Her expression became thoughtful, then she nodded. "If it'll get Mr. Oliver taken care of sooner? Absolutely."

He grinned. "Good. I'll call Clive, and let him know what I want to do."

"Clive?" Her brows rose at his easy use of the administrator's first name. "Do you think he'll agree?"

"I don't think he'll say no." Eric grinned, for once extremely grateful his grandfather's name was on the building. "Do you?"

"He might. There will be liability issues to consider."

"He won't say no." Even if *he* had to agree to fund the entire procedure. "It'll be good press for the clinic and for that fund-raiser of yours, too."

She'd told him about the masquerade ball she'd been put in charge of organizing. Not that his mother hadn't already told him a dozen times. Mostly while she simultaneously touted Ella Von Buren's many charms, including her excellent Kentucky blue-blood roots. He'd started to ask Kasey what she thought of his mother—no way could any member of the RLS not know Lena Woolworth. But he still wasn't ready to have his mother interfering in his and Kasey's relationship. Not until he felt more confident his mother wouldn't inadvertently undo the delicate threads of what Eric had worked so hard to achieve the past few weeks. Kasey's faith in him.

Kasey stopped pacing. "Good press?"

"You can use us doing this surgery as a hook to get the press to write a piece highlighting the fund-raiser. They love human-interest stuff. If Mr. Oliver prefers to remain anonymous, no names have to be used." At her open mouth, he winked. "I know a guy over in Editorial and bet we can get a front page write-up if no one gets killed or holds up a bank."

A smile spread across her face, excitement lighting her beautiful eyes. She threw her arms around his neck and kissed his cheek. "Oh, Eric, that's perfect. Thank you."

Caught off guard by her reaction, he took a step back, wrapping his arms around her to steady himself.

His arms around her soft, receptive body knocked him even more off-kilter.

As did her exuberant kiss.

It was the first time since the night they'd made love that she'd touched him of her own accord, touched him without him having first touched her.

It felt damned good. Perfect.

"If this is the thanks I get, book me for anything you like," he teased. "I'm yours to command."

She pulled back, smiling at him like he was brilliant. "Be careful, or I might take you up on that."

As if to clinch the deal, she kissed him again.

CHAPTER SEVEN

"DO YOU talk about me with Dr. Douglas?" Kasey asked Eric that night after her piano lessons. When they'd first started dating, she'd admitted to taking the lessons for two years, but that she wasn't very good. Still, she smiled when she'd talked about playing and obviously enjoyed the lessons.

Not that the opportunity had presented itself, but she'd yet to offer to play for him. Something he looked forward to as he knew she saw doing so as exposing herself.

While she'd been at her lesson, he'd eaten with his mother. A big mistake. She had invited Ella and the Von Burens. Halfway through the meal, Gladys Anderson arrived to do a piece for her gossip column. His mother had been delighted, as had the Von Burens. Eric had drawn the line at having his photo taken.

The only positive to the entire ordeal was that he and Kasey arrived at the coffee shop where they'd arranged to meet at exactly the same time. That and him confronting Gladys in front of his mother and the Von Burens on not doing her part to help the RLS. After all, she'd yet to get back in touch with Dr. Carmichael.

The woman, the Von Burens and his mother had been quite stunned. His mother had also gotten a curious gleam in her eyes that said she'd homed right in on his mention of Kasey. No doubt she'd put two and two together and realized Kasey was the woman he'd been spending his time with.

Eric had left as quickly as he could.

Rather than go inside the coffee shop, Kasey had invited him to her house so they wouldn't have to rush off as the shop closed at ten and it was already almost nine.

Trying not to read anything into the invitation, he'd driven to the trendy neighborhood of mid-sized brick houses, taking in every detail of her home with its small but immaculate yard.

"Jonathan and I talk about you occasionally," he admitted, following her into her living room. Tonight was the first time she'd invited him to her house.

Full-blooded male that he was, he wanted to whisk her off her feet and carry her over the threshold and straight to her bedroom.

She meant more to him than just sex, but every look, every touch left him wanting her more and more. Even though they had made progress, she hadn't let him inside that protective shield many had mistaken as an icy heart.

"What do you tell him?" she asked, placing her purse onto a black marble inlaid table just inside the doorway.

Eric took in the high-end furnishings that screamed success, but not much more. Not a single personal item or photograph in the entire room. He could be in a hotel suite for all the personalization. "He's curious about my relationship with you."

"And?" She stood in front of the table, looking uncertain.

He walked over to a bookshelf, glanced at the titles. All classics he'd been assigned to read throughout prep school. "Jonathan is more than a coworker. He's my best friend and has been for years. He asked me point-blank if we were involved. I wasn't going to lie to him."

"I suppose I understand that," she conceded.

"He won't say anything, if that's what worries you." He continued to take in her home. "He knows we don't want anyone at the clinic aware we're seeing other."

"Okay." She nodded. "So, Dr. Douglas knows." A nervous smile flittered across her face. "Coffee?"

The fact she didn't argue, didn't seem upset that he'd told Jonathan the truth said they'd made even more progress.

"Actually, water would be great. All this coffee late at night is interfering with my sleep."

"Oh." She bit the inside of her lip, shifted her weight. "Sorry."

She turned to go toward what he assumed was the kitchen.

He grabbed her wrist, turning her toward him. "Kasey?"

She looked at him with her big eyes. Her lips parted and she moistened them.

"I don't really want anything to drink."

She swallowed, her gaze dropping to his mouth. "What do you want?"

He ran his fingers over the bare skin of her arm until he reached the edge of the lacy camisole top she wore. "You."

She shivered, moved closer to him, stared into his eyes.

"I want you, too, Eric." The admission came freely. She wanted him. "I've wanted you from the beginning. So much I've ached."

"Thank God." He pulled her against him, kissed her lips, her throat. Slow, torturous kisses meant to tantalize, to torment, to arouse her as fully as he was, but which only succeeded in driving himself into further need.

Kasey kissed him back, matched him touch for touch, dug her fingers into his hair, his nape, his back. She slid her hands inside his shirt, up his back, pushed the tailored material off his shoulders.

"I want to touch you, Eric. All of you." Her breathy plea ripped into Eric and tore his resolve to go slow all to hell.

Dropping his shirt to the gleaming hardwood floor, he scooped her off her feet. "Where's your room?"

"That way." Burying her face into the crook of his neck, she pointed toward the hallway leading off the living room.

Tiny kisses rained over his throat. Her hot, moist tongue dipped into the groove at the base, causing him to misstep.

"Which room, Kasey?" he growled, wanting to lay her on her bed and strip her naked, feast on the way she looked waiting for him to make love to her.

She pressed another kiss to his collarbone, then lifted her head. "There."

Without setting her down, Eric fumbled in the dark until he found the light switch. Soft light flooded the peach room.

With a gentleness that almost brought tears to Kasey's eyes, he laid her on the bed, cupped her face and kissed her. With each touch, he worshipped her body, her soul.

When she lay naked before him, his eyes met hers, darkened. He dipped his head and ran his tongue over her belly in slow, sensual strokes, over and over until her entire body pulsed. Her fingers dug into the patterned quilt on her bed, bunching the material around her. He laved her navel as if branding the area as his own mark upon her body.

He moved on, loving other parts of her body, letting her finish undressing him, letting her love him in sweet exploration of their reactions to each other.

He paused to put on a condom.

Staring into her eyes, he thrust into her body, melding them into one, and all rational thought disappeared.

She sensed the longing to go faster trembling inside him like a caged beast roaring to be let loose. Yet every time she tried to increase their pace, to give him release, he reined her in with a whispered, "Not yet."

Sweat beaded on his forehead.

Lying on her with his weight partially supported on his elbows, he clasped her hands, thrust deep. Looking into his eyes, seeing the passion, seeing more, something she'd never seen in any man's eyes, Kasey had the biggest revelation of her life.

She trusted Eric.

With all her heart and all her soul. With everything she was.

Because she loved him.

And, maybe, just maybe, what she saw reflected in his eyes was love, too.

* * *

Still spiraling down from heights she'd never known, Kasey lay in Eric's arms, her ear pressed to his chest as she listened to his pounding heartbeat.

When he'd quit saying not yet, she was sure they'd left her bedroom, had floated off into Neverland or some other magic, mystical place.

Just as they had the first few times in his hotel room, they'd left the light on during their lovemaking. Part of her had felt self-conscious about doing so now that they weren't strangers, but another part had reveled in being able to see Eric, to look into his eyes and watch his reaction to her touch, his reaction to touching her.

He kissed the top or her head. "I think it's time we come out of the closet."

She lifted her head off his shoulder to look at him. "But—"

"I want to date you, Kasey. I have from the beginning. I acknowledge your fears about our working together, but I want the world to know you're mine."

Elation lifted her spirits. She rolled on top of him and smiled, her hair cascading around her head to shade their faces. "Does that mean the world will know you're mine?"

"I've been yours from the night you sat down beside me at Calista Blue's."

"You have?"

"From the moment I looked into your sad, green eyes."

Not daring to believe what she was hearing, she laughed lightly. "What man could resist?"

Which brought to mind one who had been able to resist. One Jonathan had mentioned in her office. Just how much did Eric's friend know? How much had he shared with Eric?

She rolled off him and stared up at her textured ceiling. "I was in love once."

She waited to see how he'd take her admission. Was it poor bed etiquette to reveal your past while still recovering from phenomenal sex? Probably, but it seemed imperative that she come clean about her past.

He rolled onto his side, took her hand in his and brought it to his lips. "He was a lucky man."

"He didn't think so. He dumped me for another woman." Just saying the words out loud made tears sting her eyes. "A woman with a background similar to his."

"What kind of background would that be?" Eric caressed her fingers.

"Wealthy. Old money. The kind that speaks without a nickel being spent." Kasey took a deep breath. "He came from a wealthy family just outside Nashville, where I was working at the time. So did she. Her father was on the board of trustees at the hospital where I worked in a fast-track career advancement program. After Randall and she became engaged, I was called to task for inappropriate behavior within the workplace."

Bile soured her mouth at the memories of how she'd been terminated at Skymont.

Eric remained silent, his finger tracing over hers.

"Inappropriate being that I slept with another doctor in the privacy of my home, a doctor I dated for almost a year." A wasted year of her life in so many ways. "I was given the choice of voluntarily leaving with a full recommendation or being dismissed without severance pay."

Eric sat up in the bed. "There are laws against that. You could have taken them to the cleaners."

"Sure there are laws, but who would have hired me if I'd sued, Eric?" She'd given great thought to the decisions she'd made during that time. Her natural instinct had been like Eric's: to fight. But when she'd approached the situation with logic rather than anger, she'd kept coming to the same conclusion. "Even if I'd won a lawsuit, what employer would take a risk with me? My reputation would have been ruined."

"Their reputation would have been ruined."

"Possibly, but I had more to lose than they did."

"You could have gone into practice for yourself."

"True, I could have," she admitted, had even briefly considered doing just that. Going into solo practice wouldn't have salvaged her wrecked reputation. "But my goal has always been higher than owning a private practice."

He sat in silence for a moment, before asking, "You want to replace Herbert on the medical board, don't you?"

"Yes," she admitted, relieved that he understood how important her career was to her. "I know I'm young, but my résumé is impeccable and so are my qualifications."

She glanced at Eric, unable to read his thoughtful expression. She went on. "Anyway, I wanted you to know about Randall."

"Why, Kasey? Why tell me this now? Tonight?" His terse questions surprised her.

Did he think she was trying to pressure him emotionally?

"Because I want you to understand what a risk it is

for me to be here with you, for you to understand that I didn't lightly make the decision to invite you into my bed." She tasted blood and forced her teeth to let go of her lower lip. "Because if we're going to do this, we need to be honest with each other, not have so many secrets between us."

Eric scooted up in the bed, propping pillows behind him. He studied Kasey's face, looking for any sign that she knew his secret.

The one culminating this afternoon when he'd talked to Clive about scheduling Mr. Oliver's surgery for the following morning.

Herbert had officially retired. The spot on the board was Eric's. His mother had been ecstatic.

Had Kasey somehow learned of his discussion with Clive? Was that why he was here in her bed? Why she'd told him of Randall? Of how she'd been betrayed by love?

Love.

The word brought his thoughts to a halt.

Did he love Kasey?

Certainly, he felt things for her he'd never felt before. Crazy, irrational things that made him pull strings to arrange to perform a gallbladder surgery. Things that had him thinking about the future, about the things his mother said to him about his family responsibilities.

Things like how betrayed Kasey was going to feel when she learned he'd been given the board position.

How betrayed his mother would be if he turned down the position she considered his legacy.

"I should tell you something," he began, searching

for the right place to begin and not coming up with a good start.

"You don't have to tell me," Kasey surprised him by saying. "I already know."

"You do?"

"You're from old money, too, and I know you've got inside connections with the board." She gave a breathy sigh. "Just like Randall. That's why I was scared of history repeating itself, but you're not like him."

Aw, hell. They were talking about two different things. He was talking career and she was talking heart.

Which told him quite a lot about where Kasey's feelings lay.

Unless she was manipulating him. Giving him what he wanted so he'd give her what she wanted.

Sex for the board position.

He weighed the thought in his mind, recalling how many times in the past he'd been wrong about women, about how many times he'd been used by those close to him.

Kasey was different. What they shared was different. Was something special and fragile and worth believing in, worth protecting.

"I care about you, Kasey. A lot." Telling her about the board position when they'd just made love was wrong. He couldn't let her throw her icy shield between them again. He'd find a way to tell her about Herbert, to tell her the dilemma he was in regarding the position. She'd be upset, but would understand once he explained.

Fear entered her eyes, as if she sensed a "but" coming. He didn't say it. Couldn't say it.

"I don't want to hurt you, ever."

She closed her eyes. "Then don't."

She was right. There were too many secrets between them.

"You should know it's the one thing I do well in life, hurting those I care about."

Her eyes opened, looking at him in confusion.

"When I was younger, I rebelled against my parents, did everything I could to embarrass them."

"Sounds like you were a typical teenager."

"Drugs, sex, partying, even some petty theft." At her shocked expression, he grimaced. "Not things I'm proud of, but I was still doing those things in my early twenties. I was so high at my father's funeral that I don't even recall having been there. I was a wreck."

"I'm sorry you were in such a bad place." She touched his shoulder. "You couldn't have been that bad, though, otherwise, you'd never have gotten into medical school."

"My mother bought my way into medical school."

"Bought your…?" She stopped, the enormity of what he was saying apparently sinking in. "Just how does one buy a child's way into medical school? Is that even possible? How much money would that take?"

"Apparently at that time it took enough to build a new dormitory and nursing school."

"An entire dorm and nursing school?"

Eric nodded. "It wasn't like the school was going to not let me in, was it? Much less kick me out no matter what I did when my mother funded whatever pet project they came up with."

Kasey's gasp stung.

"I didn't realize," she admitted. The shock on her face said there were a lot of things she hadn't realized. Like just how wealthy his family really was.

"Jonathan saved me."

"Dr. Douglas?" Her shock continued. "That seems…unlikely."

"He likes to have a good time, but he's never done the hard-core things I did. It wasn't until he sat me down after my father's funeral and told me to either get my act together or find a new best friend that I admitted I was on a path to self-destruction."

"Dr. Douglas did that?" Disbelief rang in her voice.

"Lots of people did, including a judge, but Jonathan was the one who got through."

"How?"

"He moved all my stuff out of our apartment and hung a wanted ad for a new best friend and roommate on the door."

"I'm…blown away."

"He's a good friend."

"Apparently." She stared at him in awe. "How did you become the wonderful doctor you are today?"

"After I went into rehab—"

"You went to rehab?" she interrupted, pulling the bedspread higher over her chest.

"I'd been doing hard drugs for months. I went to rehab." He swallowed his pride, swallowed the pain caused by the disillusionment in her eyes. "Other than the occasional alcoholic drink, I've been drug-free for seven years."

"I'm glad."

"Me, too." Eric finished telling her about how he'd turned his grades around, impressed even the most unimpressionable of his professors, known he had to do more with his life than immediately step into his father's empty shoes or the ones his mother had so nicely laid out for him to wear.

When he'd finished medical school, he'd signed up with a medical mission group and gone overseas. He'd learned to live without all the things he'd taken for granted, learned about who he was beneath the Woolworth fortune. Who he really was beneath all the spoilt layers the world saw.

It was that man who'd come home to Rivendell.

That man Eric liked looking into the mirror and seeing each day.

CHAPTER EIGHT

KASEY semi-floated the next day. Eric had stayed until just before dawn. She'd slept spooned against his hard frame only to be awakened by morning kisses.

They'd shared so much of themselves last night, revealed painful truths, clung to each other throughout the night. When she'd awakened this morning, she'd felt closer to Eric than she'd ever felt to anyone.

Because she loved him.

"You sure are perky this morning," Lora observed, grinning at Kasey. "You must be looking forward to going into surgery with Dr. Matthews."

"Must be." Kasey didn't reveal more, but the smile Lora gave her said she didn't have to. Lora recognized the glow of a woman in love.

Just as well that she and Eric had decided going public was okay. Not that they'd make an announcement or anything. She wasn't exactly sure how going public worked. She and Randall had openly dated from the beginning.

Randall. How could she have thought she wanted to

marry him? What she'd felt for him was so much less than what she felt for Eric.

Making love with Eric, knowing they'd both overcome demons, all of it was so much…more.

"There you go again," Lora teased, looking happy for Kasey. "He's a great guy."

"Yes, he is," Kasey agreed with a bright smile. "I should get to work. Who's next?"

"A new patient in room three. She wouldn't say why she's here, but she hasn't had health care in years."

"She's here through the charity fund?"

"Yes. Nice enough lady, but she gave vague answers to some of her health history questions. You may have to clarify a few items."

"Okay, guess I should get in to see her."

"Hey, Kasey?" Lora stopped her. "If you're ever free for lunch, maybe we could go to that café you like. I ate there last week and, boy, have I been missing out. Great food."

Surprised by the offer, Kasey smiled. She and Lora had grown closer over the past few weeks. She liked the nurse she suspected had feelings for Dr. Douglas. "I'd like that."

Due to the reshuffling of their schedules to clear the afternoon for Mr. Oliver's procedure, Kasey didn't see Eric until right before they headed to the surgical center.

When he met her in her office, he wore scrubs and looked dreamy. Eyes twinkling, he grinned. "Miss me?"

"Just a little," she teased, moving toward him.

He pulled her to him, holding her close. His arms felt

so good. She rested her head against his strong chest. The embrace lasted only a few seconds, but it was enough to reassure Kasey that what they'd shared during the night had been real.

He waggled his brows, checking her out. "I like your scrubs."

"I was thinking the same thing when you came in here."

"That you liked your scrubs?"

"Something like that." She laughed, wondering how in just the span of a few months she could have gone from not knowing this wonderful man to him being the center of her world.

They left her office to head toward the surgi-center.

"I spoke with Mrs. Oliver earlier," Eric told her as they stepped into the hallway. "She and her daughter are both in the waiting area. I told her we'd stop by after the surgery to let her know how everything went."

Kasey smiled. "That was thoughtful of you."

He shrugged. "They were worried about him. I wanted to reassure them."

"You know the gossip mill is buzzing about you doing this surgery, right?"

"Is it?"

She nodded. "I was too busy this morning to catch much of what was being said, but I overheard a couple of nurses talking."

He grinned. "Did they like my scrubs, too?"

"Probably." Laughing, Kasey rolled her eyes. "Is it true that you asked to work in the ambulatory clinic, but were originally supposed to have worked in a different department?"

He stopped walking, regarded her. “Does it matter?”

“Not really,” she admitted. “I was just curious as to why you would do that. Was it to work with Jonathan?”

“He is my best friend,” Eric agreed, opening the stairwell door so they could go down to the surgi-center level. When the door closed behind them, they stood on the landing. “But I’d be lying if I didn’t admit that I wasn’t thinking of Jonathan when I made the request to work in the ambulatory clinic.”

“You weren’t thinking of him?”

He shook his head.

Warmth spread through Kasey’s chest. “You wanted to work with me?”

“Under the circumstances, working together seemed like the best way to get to know you better.”

Because she’d been so adamant about not wanting anything to do with him.

“I’m sorry I pushed you away when you arrived at the clinic, Eric. I was so sure that you would think poorly of me for sleeping with you that I never gave you a chance.”

“Did you think poorly of me because I’d slept with you?”

“Sleeping with you made me think of you, but not poorly. More like with longing for a repeat.”

“Were you disappointed?”

“With the repeat? Are you kidding? Last night was amazing.” She hugged him. “You are amazing.”

“You were pretty amazing yourself.” Eric held her to him for several heartbeats. “Come on. It isn’t a good idea for us to hang around in this stairwell. Alone. Being amazed by each other. No telling what that might lead to and Mr. Oliver is waiting on us."

Together, they took the stairs, then headed toward the back of the building so they could go to the surgical center to get scrubbed.

In the sterile surgery suite, Eric maneuvered the staple gun to the correct position and clipped Mr. Oliver's gallbladder stem. Moving slightly lower, he placed another clip. When he'd secured the area, he used the laser to cut between the clips, bagging the gallbladder then pulling the stone-filled pouch free via a trochanter.

The nurse did an instrument count, a gauze count. Kasey stood on the other side of the surgery table, watching in fascination. Clear goggles shielded her eyes, a surgical mask covered her lovely face. But when her gaze met his, he knew she was smiling.

His breath caught with a blast of emotion that tightened his rib cage almost painfully.

He needed to tell her the rest of the story. About his mother. About the clinic. About how he felt about her. Tonight.

He also needed to talk to his mother, to tell her that he wouldn't risk losing Kasey over Herbert's vacant spot.

Woolworth, Inc. owned controlling stock in the clinic. If Eric wanted a position on the board, the board would create a new position. Kasey desperately wanted Herbert's spot, had set that as her marking point for success. He wouldn't deny her that success.

Turning down the position was the right thing to do.

"Would you like to do the honors?" he asked, indicating the removal of the trochanters.

Her eyes lit with excitement. "Can I?"

"Sure. You know the motto."

"The motto?"

"See one, do one, teach one," they and several of the operating room nursing staff finished in unison.

Eric demonstrated proper removal with the first trochanter and allowed Kasey to do the remaining two.

Together they secured the punctured flesh. Moments after they were finished, the nurse released where Mr. Oliver had been secured to the table to keep him from moving during surgery, and anesthesia was being reversed.

"We're finished with our part," Eric informed their groggy patient. "Now you just have to wake up well enough in Recovery that you can be put into a room so your family can visit."

Looking dazed, the man nodded, then grabbed Kasey's hand. "Thank you."

She bent down, kissed his cheek. "You're welcome, but Dr. Matthews is who really deserves your thanks. Without him, this wouldn't have happened."

They left the operating room to find Mr. Oliver's family to tell them his surgery had been a success.

"That was amazing," Kasey enthused once away from the others. Her eyes sparkled with excitement. "Enough so I think I could go back to school and do a surgical fellowship."

Eric laughed, loving the look of pure happiness on her face. Oh, yeah, he'd turn down a hundred board positions before he'd be the one to wipe the smile off her face.

The only position that really mattered was the one of being an integral part of her life.

"Let's pick up takeout and eat at your place tonight," he suggested as they walked toward the waiting room. "We can discuss your plans to make me date a college co-ed then."

She grinned, smacking his arm playfully. "Okay, so surgery might get boring if it was all I did, but being in the operating room with you was brilliant."

"Because I'm brilliant?"

"Absolutely," she agreed. "And a gifted surgeon whose talents aren't being put to full use in the ambulatory clinic."

"I like the ambulatory clinic," he reminded her.

"And I like you being in the ambulatory clinic." She shot him a look that said she liked a lot of things about him. "But perhaps the clinic isn't the best use of your many talents."

"I like the ambulatory clinic," he repeated.

"Good," she acquiesced. "We can't do takeout tonight, though. It's only two weeks until the RLS masquerade ball. I'm meeting with the ladies tonight for one last committee check-in. I mentioned it to you yesterday."

With everything that had happened over the past twenty-four hours, he'd forgotten.

Which meant she'd be dining with his mother rather than him.

Why did that put a nervous feeling in his gut?

"We need to talk before you go to your meeting, Kasey." He purposely kept his tone light, not wanting to rob her of the joy on her face. "In private."

A mischievous look came over her face. As if she thought he wanted to do something besides talk in private. Hell, he did want to. Particularly since her look wasn't one of aversion to the idea. He'd been having fantasies about that desk of hers since the first time he'd stepped into her office. Of course he'd have to turn that skeleton around. He'd swear at times the thing was watching him.

"Are we going to discuss private matters, Eric?" she teased, shooting him a flirty look.

"If you don't quit looking at me like that we're going to do more than talk." He waggled his brows.

Kasey giggled. Looking at her, Eric wondered how anyone could have ever called her an ice queen. Her smile warmed him all the way to his center.

"Tell you what," she said in a sultry tone. "Since we both have an office full of patients to see, you can reveal all your private matters tonight after I finish my meeting with the masquerade ball committee."

He didn't like waiting. Particularly not as his mother had called him this morning to check on him since he'd not come home last night. The perils of having agreed to live with her rather than in a place of his own. At the time it had seemed like a good idea since living under the same roof meant he was able to see her more. Now he knew the reasons for not living with your mother at the age of thirty-two.

"Call me after you're finished," he said, resigned that their conversation would have to wait. "I'll come over and I'm bringing clean clothes this time so I don't have to rush off in the morning."

Her eyes darkened to a deep green. Her gaze dropping to his mouth, she nodded. "I'll call the moment we're through."

Despite her happiness, Kasey fought to keep her smile that night. Doreen Von Buren once again laid into her. The woman had never been overly friendly. Overly friendly wasn't the RLS style, but never had Kasey felt so blatantly attacked. From a woman she'd long admired from afar.

"You haven't talked to the florist?" Doreen snapped. "What are you thinking? The ball is in less than a fortnight. We'll end up with weeds on the tables if you don't get with the program."

"I'm not handling the floral arrangements. Daphne Moore is," Kasey said through a clenched teeth smile.

"Daphne?" Doreen glanced around the table, but Daphne hadn't shown that evening. "Well, then, I'm sure it's been taken care of."

"I'm sure." Kasey mentally added calling the florist to her list of things to do. Just in case.

Doreen made a snide remark about incompetent hired help beneath her breath.

Hired help? Kasey opened her mouth to confront the woman. She'd had enough. But before a sound came out of her mouth, someone else spoke up.

"Kasey has been volunteering with our group for several years and has recently been given status as a junior member." The classically beautiful woman sitting at the head of the table commented with her usual elegance and grace. She'd been sitting quietly, as had the other five women, watching the exchange. “On whatever level she’s served, Kasey has always gone above and beyond to make sure our events are successful. I’m sure the masquerade ball will be no exception.”

She hadn’t realized the RLS matron had noticed all the hard work she’d done for the group since she’d moved to Rivendell.

With those simple words from Lena Woolworth the room suddenly found everything Kasey had done or suggested to be utterly brilliant.

Well, Doreen didn’t find her utterly brilliant. Doreen glowered, but she didn’t speak another unsavory word. Not even a veiled one.

The committee adjourned. Kasey gathered her purse from where she’d tucked it beside her chair. When she rose, Lena said, “Kasey, be a dear and walk with me to wait on my car. I’d like to discuss something in private.”

“Yes, ma’am.” A bevy of nerves rushed through Kasey. Was Lena going to invite her to become a fully fledged RLS member? Surely not this soon? There were other volunteers who’d been junior members far longer than Kasey had been living in Rivendell.

When they stepped outside the restaurant, Lena handed the valet her ticket stub and turned to Kasey. “I have a favor to ask.”

A favor? Kasey fought to keep her surprise hidden. “You must know I believe in the work the RLS does and would help in any way that I can.”

Lena smiled with her usual regal elegance. “I’m pleased to hear that, but this is personal.”

Personal?

Lena watched her closely, expectantly. "It involves my son."

"Your son?" Not long after joining the RLS she'd heard Lena had a son, but that he didn't live in Kentucky. Had he returned home? Did he need medical assistance?

"Yes, I'd like you to convince him to attend the fundraiser." Lena watched her closely. "Our family is being honored during the ball. He should be there."

Kasey couldn't imagine not wanting to take advantage of an opportunity to be proud of one's family's accomplishments. What was wrong with Lena's son? "Why wouldn't he want to be there when his family is being honored?"

Lena laughed, her lovely eyes still fixated on Kasey. "It's a long story, but suffice it to say that my son marches to the beat of his own drum."

Probably a spoilt kid who had no clue how good he had it.

"I'll do what I can and attempt to convince him." How, she had no clue, but this was a personal favor for Lena Woolworth. How often did that happen in one's lifetime? No way would she say no. "But wouldn't it be more effective to ask someone who actually knows him?"

Lena laughed again in that sparkly way she had. "But, darling, you do know him. Eric mentioned you while at we were having dinner with Ella and her parents. I did a little checking." The woman's eyes twinkled with a light that hinted she'd done more than a little checking. "You work in the same clinic as my Eric."

Eric. As in…

"Dr. Matthews is your son? I thought your son was

younger. In his early twenties." That was the impression she'd gotten from the few things she'd heard about Lena's son. Young and irresponsible.

Eric was Lena Woolworth's son.

Eric had had dinner with Ella? The thought almost blindsided Kasey as much as the news that he was Lena's son. She couldn't be more dazed if Lena had struck her head with a baseball bat and stars danced before her eyes.

Eric had never said anything about them being exclusive to each other. She'd just assumed.

He'd had dinner with Ella. And his mother.

Hadn't Kasey once thought he'd eventually want someone like Ella?

Taking measure of Kasey's reaction, Lena smiled. "I know it must be surprising to discover I have a son in his thirties, but time does slip by." She gave another mysterious smile. "I was extremely young when I married Frank."

How had she not put two and two together? Then again, why would she have assumed Eric Matthews was the young and rebellious Woolworth heir she'd occasionally heard tell of?

Why would she assume that the wonderfully, responsible man she'd fallen in love with was the son of the woman who owned controlling stock in the clinic where they worked?

After all, Eric had known for weeks she was a junior member of the RLS.

Hadn't she even mentioned some of the ladies by name? Mentioned his *mother* by name?

He'd never said anything.

Not once had he pointed out that she'd been meeting with his mother.

Because, despite everything he'd said, Kasey Carmichael wasn't good enough to take home and introduce to his mother.

He had Ella for dinners with his mother.

When it came down to it, Eric wanted her for sex. Nothing more.

Just like Randall.

CHAPTER NINE

WHEN Eric arrived at the clinic the next morning, he stopped by Kasey's office first thing. As they'd arranged, she'd called the night before while driving home from her gathering with the RLS. But she'd begged off meeting him, claiming a headache.

She'd denied that anything more was wrong. He'd offered to come over and take care of her, but she'd insisted she just needed to get a good night's rest to get rid of the headache.

A headache? Couldn't she have come up with something more original?

He'd ended up going to Jonathan's and shooting a few games of pool. They'd shot the breeze until the early morning hours.

Despite the fact he'd gotten very little sleep, Eric had arrived at the clinic early.

Kasey's office door stood open, but she wasn't there. Just that damned skeleton that he'd swear guarded the room.

"Looking for Kase?" Jonathan asked from behind him.

Shaking his head, he turned. "You've seen her this morning?"

"Briefly. She went into an exam room a few minutes ago."

He'd hoped to catch her before she got started, but she must have come in early, too.

Jonathan regarded Eric with crossed arms. "Did you talk to her last night?"

He eyed his friend. "It was late when I left your place. Surely you didn't think I'd call her after midnight? If she did have a headache, and I woke her, she'd be upset."

"Rightly so." Jonathan agreed. "But it wouldn't surprise me to hear you had called. Or gone on over to her place. You've got it bad."

Eric didn't deny his friend's claim. He'd admitted as much the night before.

"What did your mother say this morning?" Jonathan asked. "I can't imagine she's thrilled that you're dating someone who grew up in the projects. Or is Lena so happy to have you home she doesn't care who you're involved with?"

Eric had no illusions that his mother cared a great deal. As her only child and sole heir, she'd always felt she had more say in his life than he did. Despite his mother's philanthropic work to better the plight of the poor, she was an elitist in many ways.

"She wasn't out of bed when I left this morning. Like I said last night, I have mentioned Kasey to my mother. I didn't tell her we were involved, though. Just that one of her junior RLS members worked at the clinic with me."

"You've been walking around whistling Dixie, you

think Lena hasn't noticed?" Jonathan snorted. "You took a woman to the Wild W for a private picnic. You failed to come home the other night. You think Lena didn't immediately jump to all the right conclusions when you mentioned Kasey?"

Eric grinned self-derisively. "Since she backed off throwing Ella Von Buren in my face after I mentioned Kasey, I'm sure she did."

"Ella? Wasn't she on the cover of that women's magazine a few months ago?" Jonathan whistled with appreciation. "Tell you what, your mother can throw Ella my way. I should be so lucky."

Eric shrugged. "Deal, but I'll warn you, she's more looks than brain."

"Just how I like them," Jonathan bragged, earning a laugh from Eric.

Kasey stepped out of the exam room, spotted the two of them talking, and smiled. A polite smile that didn't reach her tired-appearing eyes.

Eric's stomach knotted. Something was wrong. What had happened from the time he'd kissed her goodbye yesterday evening to when she'd called him to cancel?

His mother.

"Good morning, Eric. Dr. Douglas." She didn't meet Eric's eyes; instead she smiled at Jonathan.

"Jonathan," his friend insisted. "Call me Jon-a-than."

Kasey nodded and stepped past them into her office.

With a go-get-'em-tiger grin, Jonathan slugged him on the shoulder, then disappeared into a patient room. Eric followed Kasey into her office and closed the door behind him.

He avoided looking at Bones. "Feel better this morning?"

The blank look that briefly passed over her face said more than her words, confirming his suspicions.

"Yes, much," she recovered. "Thanks for asking."

She'd lied to him about her headache. To get out of seeing him last night.

Eric didn't like games. Never had. "What's going on? I thought we'd moved past this."

Kasey backed up against her desk, but didn't sit. "This?"

"You think I can't look at you and see that something's wrong? Yesterday you lit up when you saw me," he pointed out. "Today you practically cringed."

"I just have a lot on my plate right now." She didn't deny the cringe, which slam-dunked his stomach with doubts of where they stood with each other.

"With this masquerade ball," she continued, not looking at him. "Please understand."

Could her distance really be that simple?

He'd never organized a masquerade, but his mother had many times over the years. He'd never seen her stress one. Of course, Lena never stressed such things. She had plenty of minions to take care of the details and the stress.

But Kasey did look stressed. Then again, Kasey was one of his mother's minions.

Hell, he'd tell his mother to lay off Kasey, to get some of her minions to lighten Kasey's load. Whatever it took to ease the tension from her face.

But the real question was what had his mother told Kasey?

"What did she say to you?"

Kasey's face paled. "Who?"

He sank back against the cabinet, bumped into the creepy skeleton, then straightened. "My mother."

"Why would you ask me about your mother, Eric?" Kasey's eyes narrowed. "You've never even introduced me to your mother."

"Is that why you're upset? That I never introduced you to Lena?" He'd been protecting her, but it struck him that Kasey might see him not introducing her in a bad light.

"I couldn't care less that you didn't introduce me." She straightened the skeleton he'd bumped, her voice so flat it conveyed more emotion than if she'd screamed at him.

"I can see that."

What he saw was the anger sparking in Kasey's green eyes. And the hurt. And the sheer determination.

She pinned him beneath her intent gaze. "Were you serious about us going public that we're a couple?" she surprised him by asking. "If so, you'll go with me to the masquerade ball."

His mother had been trying to get him to commit for weeks, but he'd held off. He wasn't overly fond of such occasions, this one more than most. But if Kasey wanted him to escort her to the ball, he'd be honored.

What did Kasey want? Him? His name? His money? Did the social ladder matter to her as much as she sometimes let on?

"Fine, I'll go to the ball with you."

The challenge in her eyes momentarily shifted. "You'll come to the masquerade ball as my date?"

At her surprise, he asked, "Did you think I wouldn't?"

"Actually…" She let the word draw out. "I thought you might already have a date for the evening."

Why would she think that?

"The only plans I have with any woman are with you, Kasey."

She placed her finger against her chin and pretended thoughtfulness. "Gee, and I thought you'd had dinner with another woman."

Oh, yeah. His mother had been talking. "My mother?"

Kasey's eyes narrowed. "Ella Von Buren."

"She was my mother's guest. Not mine."

"Right."

Why did he feel as if he was on trial?

"I'm telling you the truth," he said simply. He was not going to argue with her about Ella. He'd done nothing wrong and wouldn't defend himself as if he had.

"Fine." Kasey shrugged as if it were no big deal. "You're telling the truth."

She stood a few feet away looking at him with impassive eyes. Impassive eyes that hid whatever was really going on inside her head.

"And?" he prompted when she didn't say more.

"You know the old saying."

Eric had no idea what she was talking about. "What saying would that be?"

"The truth shall set you free."

What she was saying, implying, sank in. Stunned him.

"You don't want to see me anymore?" Two nights ago she'd made love with him and now she was dumping him? "Didn't you just invite me to go to the fundraiser with you?"

"I wasn't expecting you to agree to go," she said in a rushed tone, her chest rising and falling in a deep breath. "I'm sorry, Eric. But more and more this is feeling like the past come back to haunt me."

"I'm not like Randall."

"So you keep saying." Kasey turned, the light illuminating the smudges beneath her eyes that said she hadn't slept well the night before. "But let's look at the facts." She paced three steps to the wall and turned back toward him. "You are from old money, work at the same place I do, and failed to acknowledge our relationship to your family." She ticked the items off on her fingers. "Sounds similar to me."

"We agreed to keep our relationship private," he reminded her, moving closer to her, but she backed away, her back pressing against the wall. "I was honoring that agreement."

"Nice," she said with a sarcastic twist to her voice. "It must be great to be able to ease your conscience by saying you were doing me a favor by not acknowledging my existence in your life."

"I told Jonathan," he said.

Kasey snorted. "Bragging about your latest conquest to your best friend doesn't count."

Kasey wasn't just venting anger. She was serious. Eric sighed, wishing he knew the right words to say to make her understand how he felt. "You weren't my latest conquest, Kasey."

"Oh?" A dark brow rose. "You've already moved on to someone else? Perhaps Ella is your latest conquest?" she bit out, a toothpaste-ad smile on her face. "And good news, she comes from good breeding stock and apparently already has your mother's blessing."

Eric crossed his arms, refusing to take her bait. "I haven't done anything wrong."

"Do you really believe that?" She laughed, raking her gaze over him. "Perhaps you do. A rich, spoiled man as yourself has no clue what honor and loyalty mean."

"Do you really believe that?" He tossed her accusation back at her, but her expression remained stoic. "You're being unreasonable, Kasey."

"Do you want to know what's unreasonable, Eric?" She took a step toward him, pointed her finger at his chest, emphasizing her words. "What's unreasonable is that I thought you were different." She poked her finger into his sternum. "What's unreasonable is that you knew I was meeting with your mother once a week and you failed to say anything."

She was right. He should have told her about his mother, introduced them. How could he explain about Lena's personality?

She jabbed her finger hard against his chest. "What's unreasonable is that I thought we were involved in a monogamous relationship and all the while you were wooing Ella on the side."

He opened his mouth to correct her, but she rushed on.

"What's unreasonable is that until you showed up I thought I was a shoo-in for the medical board position, but the truth is I never had a shot because it's always been yours."

Now still wasn't a good time to tell her about Clive offering him the position.

Because she was right about that, too.

With him out of the picture, she was a shoo-in for the promotion.

"If the position hadn't already been yours, Mommy dearest could always buy you a spot on the board." Kasey hit below the belt, but she didn't look remorseful. She looked like she'd like to physically hit him to go along with her emotional punch. "The board should play their cards right. The clinic could end up with a new wing."

"Don't say things you're going to regret," he warned, knowing she was speaking from anger and hurt. But her words cut deep. Cut to the part of him that had sent him over the edge so many years ago. The part of him that he'd shed while in Africa.

"Stop and think about what you're doing."

"I am thinking about what I'm doing," she insisted. "We come from different worlds. And I'm not just talking about financially. What you did was wrong."

What he'd done? What had he done? Save her from his mother's bulldozing? Cared about her? "You really are being unreasonable."

"What's unreasonable," she continued, picking back up with her earlier train of thought, stabbing at his chest, "is that I believed in you, trusted you with my heart and invited you into my bedroom. Good thing I've seen reason." She stood a few inches taller, her chin thrust forward and her eyes sparkling. "Because what is reasonable is that we are through."

"No." He wasn't going to let her relegate him to being pushed aside at the first sign of trouble. "You're not leaving." He stood firmly in front of her, blocking her exit from the office. "You're going to talk to me. Right now."

"You want to talk?" Acid dripped from her tongue. "Fine, let's talk about how nice it must be to have everything in life handed to you on a silver platter."

"Kasey—"

"But guess what?" she interrupted, pushing against his chest. "You can't have everything, Eric. Because you can't have me. Not anymore. Not ever again."

A cold sweat popped onto his skin. Spears of emotion twisted into his gut. She was seriously calling them quits.

"I've already lost one job due to inappropriate behavior with a man." She glared at him, daggers of her hatred lancing his heart. "You might have your family name to insure your job, but I don't. Goodbye, Eric."

Dazed, Eric stood in Kasey's office, wondering what the hell had just happened and how things had gotten so out of control.

She'd dumped him.

Because he hadn't introduced her to his mother?

Because he'd had dinner with Ella?

No, their problems went deeper than that.

Much deeper.

The real problem lay with the fact that she didn't trust him, that she lumped him into the same category as her ex.

As if he hadn't done everything possible to earn her trust.

Had he been so wrong about her? He'd thought she saw the real him. The him he'd found in Africa. The him he was proud of. Instead, she saw the old him, the him who might have deserved being rejected.

A knock sounded on Kasey's office door, then, without waiting for a response, Jonathan entered the room.

"I'd ask how your talk with Kasey went, but I heard. For that matter, the entire office heard when she slammed the door in your face. I've never seen her so upset," Jonathan pointed out with a low whistle. "Actually, I've never seen her upset, period. What did you say to her to set her off like that?"

Eric picked up the skeleton's hand and let it drop back to its side. The bony fingers rattled against the skeleton's hip.

What had he said?

He'd gone into her office intent on clearing the air between them. Was that what he'd done? Cleared the air? Because there was a horrible stench floating about. One that reeked of being given the heave-ho.

The stench of him being hurt by Kasey not trusting him. After all this time, she didn't trust him.

He took a deep breath.

"I have to admit I'm surprised at you," Jonathan mused in Eric's continued silence.

Eric glanced at his friend. "Why?"

"Because you never set Kasey straight."

"I told her she was being unreasonable."

"Telling an upset woman she's being unreasonable—isn't that the same as waving a red cape in front of a bull?"

"Says the man who's never had a serious relationship with a woman." Was he being defensive? Most likely, but obviously Jonathan had no clue what he was talking about. Not when it came to Kasey. After all, once upon a time his friend had called her the Ice Queen. That alone proved how little he knew about Kasey.

"Hey, that isn't so," Jonathan denied. "Every woman I've been involved with has been a serious relationship. I've loved 'em, every one." He leaned back against Kasey's desk, his legs crossed at his ankles. "Why didn't you tell her about Lena? Why didn't you make her see 'reason'?"

"She stormed out of here before I could." Literally, she'd stormed out of her office on a cloud of righteous indignation.

"Really?" Jonathan played devil's advocate. "If Kasey was important to you, really important to you, you'd have made her listen, made her see reason. You'd have made her hear what you were saying."

"Just like you're hearing what I'm saying."

"Look." Jonathan uncrossed his legs, stood. "All I'm saying is that Kasey has a point. You've been sneaking around with her for weeks, never mentioning that she was serving on a committee with your mother. That doesn't bode well with any woman. Much less one as highly strung as Kasey Carmichael."

Jonathan had never steered him wrong. Had always laid it out straight. Even when it wasn't what Eric wanted to hear.

"Fine." Eric straightened, shoving his hands into his pants pockets. "I'll go make her listen."

Jonathan shook his head. "Not during office hours. Wait until the patients are seen, then make her listen if that's what you want. Kasey isn't the kind of woman to appreciate the drama of having her private affairs aired in her workplace."

Damn it, Jonathan was right.

"I've never seen you this torn up over a woman. If she's what you want, if you trust her motives, you better figure it out before you have that discussion."

Eric raked his fingers through his hair, eyeing his friend as if he had no clue who he was. "When the hell did you get so smart?"

Jonathan grinned, socked his arm. "I've always been this smart. You just now figuring that out?"

Kasey finished her day without additional run-ins with Eric. Not that she'd been able to avoid seeing him, but she had managed to avoid being cornered.

Which was a huge relief.

When she'd slammed out of her office, her gaze had immediately landed on Lora and Jonathan standing in the hallway.

She'd gone red-faced in shame.

The guilty look on Lora's face had said they'd heard it all. Everything she and Eric had said to one another.

Mortification hit Kasey.

Mortification like she hadn't felt since her mother had shown up drunk at her graduation ceremony and left in the backseat of a police car.

But Kasey kept her head high and went into the room where her next patient waited.

All day, she kept her head high, her smile in place, and she successfully avoided Eric.

Mostly because she got the impression he was avoiding her, too.

Which hurt.

She'd been right about him all along.

He'd gotten what he wanted a couple of nights ago, and now they were through.

She may have beaten him to the punch, called an end before he did, but Eric hadn't put up a fight.

No, he may have looked stunned, but he hadn't stopped her, hadn't given her explanations of why he'd made the choices he had regarding their relationship.

Because he'd never considered her worth the effort.

Which didn't quite ring true, but her heart ached too much to give full credence to her niggles of doubt.

When she said goodbye to her last patient for the day, Kasey bumped into Clive Evans. The administrator had been lingering outside her office.

Had he been waiting for her?

Why would the administrator be waiting on her?

Had word gotten out about her argument with Eric?

Panic seized her, cut off her air supply. The room spun, causing her to reach out to touch the wall to regain her balance.

Their disagreement had only been that morning. Had Eric already put pressure on the administrator to let her go?

Just as Skymont had?

Kasey lifted her chin.

She wasn't leaving her job at Rivendell. Not without a fight.

A fight the likes of which Rivendell had never seen.

The likes of which Dr. Eric Matthews had never seen.

Determined to be strong, she opened her office door and waited for Mr. Evans to be seated. "What can I do for you, Mr. Evans?"

Her brain raced ahead. She'd hire a lawyer. The best lawyer in Rivendell. In Kentucky.

She'd take the case all the way. To the Supreme Court if she had to.

If Eric thought he could get away with this, he was wrong.

She would fight him.

Mr. Evans looked smug with the news he'd come to deliver. Probably enjoying being one of Eric's gofers. "I came to talk to you regarding the board position being vacated by Dr. Herbert retiring."

Kasey inhaled sharply. The board position? Had Eric sent the administrator to break the news to her?

"What about the board position?" she asked cautiously, wondering why Eric hadn't told her himself. It wasn't as if she didn't already know.

"We'd like to unofficially extend the position to you."

Sure she'd heard wrong, Kasey stared at the lanky man. "Me? You're sure?"

He laughed. "I'm sure, but I have to admit that's not how I expected you to respond."

"I'm a bit stunned, sir." Stunned didn't begin to cover it. She was floored. Blown away. She'd been expecting a battle to keep her job. Not a promotion.

"In a good way, I presume?" her boss asked.

"Of course." She pulled her racing thoughts together. "As I'd mentioned when I interviewed with Rivendell, a seat on the medical board has always been my goal."

"Yes, your high aspirations helped make you stand out from a few of the other qualified physicians we spoke with before hiring you."

Kasey really couldn't believe her ears. She was being offered the board position. Not Eric. How had that happened?

Had someone on the board slipped?

Would Lena be so upset she'd stop funding the charity providing care through the clinic? That would break Kasey's heart as the ramifications would affect so many. Actually, if she knew that's what would happen, that people like Mr. Oliver would be denied health care, she'd let Eric have the position.

"Sir, I'm pleased, but I must admit I'm surprised Dr. Matthews isn't being offered the position."

Mr. Evans's eyes flashed with surprise at her gutsy comment. They also flashed with something more. Something Kasey couldn't label, yet instinctively knew what it was.

"He was offered the position, wasn't he?" she guessed, her heartbeat increasing in tempo.

Mr. Evans met her gaze. "The clinic is fortunate to have a doctor like Dr. Matthews. But the clinic is also fortunate to have a doctor like you. You're being offered the board position, Dr. Carmichael."

An evasive answer any politician would be proud of. If not for her strong suspicions her puffed-up ego would be lifting her body off the ground. She was suspicious, though.

"Was Dr. Matthews offered the board position?" she demanded, her voice no-nonsense.

The administrator's face contorted into a tight mask. "You are not privy to certain items of business related to the running of this facility."

Another evasive answer.

"You offered him the position and he turned it down." It wasn't a question, but an answer to the question she'd asked. "Why?"

"Dr. Carmichael, I find your reaction to a tremendous opportunity for advancement within this clinic entirely inappropriate."

Inappropriate.

How she hated that word.

How it grated with the past.

"I would advise you to quit looking a gift horse in the mouth and appreciate the opportunity you've been handed," he continued. "Anything else is entirely inappropriate."

Could he have made a more appropriate word choice?

Inappropriate.

The only inappropriateness was that she'd opened her heart to Eric, allowed him into her life. She'd trusted him.

How inappropriate.

CHAPTER TEN

WITHOUT preamble, Kasey barged into Eric's office. "How dare you try to manipulate me this way?"

Looking way too professional and calm, he looked up from what he'd been working on. "Manipulate you?"

"Don't play dumb with me," she warned, crossing over to stand in front of his desk. "You know exactly what I mean."

"This isn't about my mother?"

She paused a moment, giving thought to his question. "No, this has nothing to do with your mother. At least, I don't think so."

"Then what?"

She wanted to strangle him for playing innocent. Of all things, Eric wasn't innocent. He'd used her, manipulated her, was still manipulating her, although she hadn't worked out his reasons. "I know what you did, Eric."

He set his pen down on his desk, leaned back in his leather chair and regarded her. "I've done lots of things during my lifetime. You'll have to be more specific."

She heaved a frustrated sigh. "I know you turned down the board position."

He considered her a few moments, not answering her one way or the other. "Why would you think that?"

"Why?" she scoffed. "Because I was offered the position a few minutes ago."

"Congratulations."

"Congratulations?" she stormed, wanting to slam her fist down on his desk. "You think I took the position? When I knew the only reason it was offered to me was because you'd turned it down? That I was second best?"

"You aren't second best, Kasey."

"Darn straight I'm not," she agreed, losing some of the wind of her anger. Why was he being so nice? She didn't want nice, she realized. She wanted emotion from him. Passion. She wanted evidence that he cared. "Why would you turn down the board position?"

"Because the position meant more to you than it did to me."

His gaze met hers and she got a glimmer of something. Not passion, but something.

"I'm not taking your leftovers."

Leftovers? Not how most people would consider a lucrative spot on the Rivendell Medical Center's medical board.

"Don't cut off your nose to spite your face, Kasey."

"Don't spout clichés at me."

"You wanted the spot on the board, it's yours."

An invisible hand reached up from her belly, locked on to her throat and gave a powerful yank downward.

"I turned the position down."

"Easily remedied. Tell Clive you've changed your mind."

"I won't be changing my mind." She wouldn't. She'd been wrong about Eric. But obviously he was wrong about her, too. "I didn't sleep with you to advance my career."

"I never said you did."

"But that's what's happening, isn't it?"

"No."

"You turned down the position because of what I told you the other night. Because of what happened with Randall."

"Yes." He smiled, apparently pleased she was starting to understand where he was coming from.

"Would you have turned down the position if we weren't involved?"

"That's a silly question. We are involved."

"Answer me. Would you have sent Mr. Evans to me if we weren't lovers?"

"Technically, we aren't lovers. You dumped me this morning."

"Did you turn down the position hoping we'd get back together?"

"I enjoy our time together, Kasey. I wasn't happy when you refused to meet me last night."

"Because you wanted to have sex with me again?"

"I've been waiting to have sex with you again from the moment we met."

She wouldn't be manipulated this way. She'd thought the manipulation was going to be directed at pushing her out of the clinic. Instead it was the opposite. Eric was trying to manipulate her into a sexual relationship with him.

Neither was going to work.

"Nothing's changed. I meant what I said this morning. We're through, Eric." They'd tried, but it was obvious that they couldn't overcome their differences. She wouldn't have to go through life condemning herself for not attempting to make things work with Eric. She had, but he'd already had future plans.

"You're upset I turned down the position?" He gawked at her, disbelief on his face. "I did it for you, Kasey. Because you wanted the position."

"Not like this, I don't."

"Whoever said a man couldn't please a woman was damned right." He stood up, walking across the room in agitation. "I never know where I stand with you. You say you want the position, I give it to you and you hold that against me."

"Gave it to me? You didn't think I'd have a problem with that? Unlike some, I want to earn my way."

"It really burns you up that I didn't live in poverty as a child, doesn't it? That's the real issue here. That you want to punish me for having wealth, a family, for having what you didn't. Sorry, Kasey, but I'm not going to take that punishment."

"You have no idea what you're talking about."

"Sure, I don't." His brown eyes darkened and his lips pursed. "I planned to talk to you tonight, planned to explain about my mother, but there's really not any point, is there, Kasey? You've condemned me without a trial. No matter what I say or do, you're never going to trust me with your heart."

A week and a half later on the evening of the masquerade ball, Kasey buzzed around the banquet hall making last-minute checks. The caterers had arrived on time and set up a delicious spread. The florists had done gorgeous arrangements for each of the tables scattered around the room. The beautiful bouquets of fresh flowers that graced the tables right inside the hotel ballroom smelled so heavenly they'd almost taken her breath away when she'd passed by. The sound system had been checked and double-checked. The emcee, a local television news personality, had arrived moments ago for any last-minute updates on his duties.

All in all, she'd done everything she could to ensure the evening's success. For the RLS and personally.

She'd scheduled an appointment with Lora's sister who worked as a hairstylist in a nearby salon. Lora had insisted that she let Tracy do her makeup, too. Kasey had. Although heavier than normal, Kasey liked how the smoky colors made her eyes appear huge.

Eyes that were no longer hidden behind glasses thanks to the contact lenses she'd purchased earlier in the week. She hadn't quite adjusted to the feel of them yet, but no longer felt as if she had an eyelash in her eye.

Careful not to disturb her fancy hairdo or makeup, Kasey had donned her rented princess gown from a costume shop. She'd reserved the gown several weeks ago before Eric had started at the clinic. She'd even found "glass" slippers to wear with the gown. A dainty white silk purse and a dab of perfume completed her look for the evening.

With her gown, makeup, hair and contact lenses, she felt so much like Cinderella she wished she could orchestrate a magic pumpkin carriage to whisk her off to the ball. But that would have meant she thought her Prince Charming was waiting for her to arrive.

Perhaps he was.

God, she hoped he was.

Guests began arriving and the room quickly filled to near capacity. The noise level from numerous conversations drowned out the soft music playing in the background.

Kasey bumped into a couple of her coworkers, who praised her outfit and hair. When she walked away she could still hear them commenting on her costume.

"Kasey?" Lora came up beside her. "Wow. You look fabulous! I hope you don't mind if I tell everyone Tracy did your hair and makeup. She could use the business. When folks get a load of you, they're going to be beating her door down."

"If you think it'll help her, go ahead. She did a wonderful job." Kasey touched one of the upswept curls on top of her head. Rather than the tightly pulled-back look she usually wore, Tracy had created a loose mass of curls that framed Kasey's face. A few stray tendrils tickled the nape of her neck and a sparkly tiara framed the front.

"You and the RLS ladies really outdid yourself on this." Lora spread her arm out, indicating the packed ballroom.

Kasey's gaze lit on where Eric, dressed as Prince

Charming, stood talking to the administrator and a couple of members from the clinic's board. Kasey had met them. But she'd never relaxed around them. They'd reminded her too closely of the jerks she'd had to deal with at Skymont.

Eric glanced up, caught sight of her. Pausing in mid-sentence, he lifted his hand to his heart, causing several of his companions to turn to see what had caught his attention. Letting his gaze caress over every feature, he ate her up with his eyes. He didn't hide the possessiveness in his expression, didn't hide the pure desire on his face.

But he made no move toward her.

He wouldn't.

He'd made his stance clear.

He'd laid his cards on the table. She didn't trust him. He found that unacceptable. The next move would have to be hers.

Their eyes clashed.

Kasey's feet stuck to the floor, and she couldn't move. In that moment, with her eyes locked with Eric's, everyone else in the room faded.

She loved him. Why else would her heart have shattered? The question came down to whether she trusted him. Did she trust him not to hurt her?

She'd thought so on the night they'd made love in her bed. She still thought so. So why had she been so quick to end their relationship?

One truth stood out. Not telling Eric how she felt was selfish, would truly put her in the same league as her mother as no other act could.

Eric turned back to the men he was talking to, resuming his conversation without another glance her way.

"You're wasting your time," Doreen Von Buren said, sliding up next to Kasey and following her gaze. "Men like Eric Matthews want their cake and to eat it, too. You're just this month's flavor."

"Pardon?" Not that Kasey was sure she wanted to know what Doreen meant. She suspected she didn't.

"Don't play coy. I saw you at Barnaby's with him about a month ago and decided to do a background check."

Had anyone not done a background check on her?

"A good thing I did, too. You're nothing more than a gold-digging tramp."

Kasey's mouth dropped. "Excuse me?"

"You heard me." Doreen took a long drink from her wineglass. "You've always had your sights set on marrying well."

"You know this how?"

"Randall Covington III," Doreen bit out with a snide smile. "He was more than willing to tell me anything I wanted to know. I passed on his words of advice to Eric."

"What words of advice?"

"That he should be careful or you'd be knocked up before he could say hefty child support." Doreen smiled with snobby finesse.

Drawing upon years of experience at hiding her emotions, Kasey gave a tight smile. "I hope you had a pleasant visit with Randall. Now, if you'll excuse me."

She didn't want to make a scene at the fund-raiser she'd spent so much time organizing. More and more she was thinking she didn't like the women she'd long admired. That perhaps those women weren't so different from the ones her mother had hung out with, only they had more money to mask their flaws.

She did believe in the work the RLS did, though, particularly in the funding of health care for the uninsured. For that reason alone, she'd remain pleasant.

Doreen grabbed Kasey's arm. "Don't walk away from me, you little tramp."

Kasey's gaze dropped to where Doreen grasped her arm.

"That's twice tonight you've called me a name." Smiling brightly in case anyone was looking their way, Kasey tipped Doreen's wineglass over. The liquid poured down the front of Doreen's flapper dress. "You really should be more careful. I bite back."

Okay, so maybe dumping your drink down someone's dress wasn't being pleasant, but Kasey felt quite pleased.

She turned and walked away, her head held high. She'd not gone ten feet when she bumped into Lena.

"Your cheeks are red, dear. Are you feeling under the weather?" Eric's mother asked in such a tone that her accent sounded more British than Southern. To go with the modified accent, Lena was dressed as the Queen of England.

"I'm fine." Other than she'd just poured wine down Doreen Von Buren's dress. No big deal. But, oh, had standing up to the woman felt good. "Just a tad nervous about how everything is going."

"Based on every seat being sold and the donation boxes at the front of the room being stuffed, I'd say everything is going splendidly," Lena praised. "That is a lovely gown, dear. You're Cinderella?"

Kasey nodded, watching from the corner of her eye as Doreen stomped out of the ballroom, the long scarlet feather in her headband flapping with each flounce.

"Perhaps before the stroke of midnight you'll dance with Prince Charming."

Kasey's gaze returned to Eric's mother, trying to read her expression. "Perhaps."

"I'm not sure how much my son has told you, but I almost lost him about eight years ago."

Under the circumstances, talking about Eric with his mother didn't feel right, but Kasey didn't step away. She couldn't. "Lost him?"

"To drugs and a reckless lifestyle. My husband loved the power of the corporate world and from the time Eric was born he pushed Eric. They clashed terribly. I often wonder if Eric didn't initially get involved with the wrong crowd just to strike out at his father."

"Why would he do that?"

"Because he forced a lifestyle on Eric that he didn't want."

"Pardon me for saying it, but the lifestyle you lead isn't a burden by any stretch."

"Don't you believe it," Lena contradicted, her sharp gaze cutting into Kasey. "Eric's father worked from dawn till the midnight hours. By choice, but that didn't make any difference to a son who wanted his father's attention."

"Eric rebelled to get his father's attention?"

"You didn't think he did it because he wasn't intelligent enough to know better?"

"No," Kasey admitted cautiously, wondering where their conversation was headed. Wondering why they were even having this conversation.

"Eric didn't choose his father's world, but mine didn't fit either. Wealth carries great responsibility to society. It also carries the constant gaze of the public eye. Not everyone is equipped to deal with those stressors."

"You think Eric isn't?"

"Eric is equipped to deal with anything he chooses. When Frank died, Eric plunged so low that nothing I did could lift him. But he got past that, left Kentucky and grew into a man any mother could be proud of." Lena's gaze held Kasey mesmerized. "As much as a mother is grateful for parental pride, what she wants more than anything is for her child to be happy."

What did Lena expect her to say? Kasey wanted Eric to be happy, too. He deserved happiness.

"I love my son. Very much. There's little I wouldn't do to make him happy. Little I wouldn't destroy that threatened his happiness."

Was that encouragement or a warning?

"He's very lucky to have you." How had she gotten into a conversation about Eric with his mother? "If you'll excuse me…" she smiled at Lena "…I need to check on the emcee."

Before Lena could stop her, Kasey headed to the opposite side of the room and came face-to-face with Eric and Ella Von Buren. Great. The night just kept getting better and better.

Looking remarkably like Marilyn Monroe, Ella flirted

outrageously with Eric, right down to running her finger along the front of his ruffled shirt and leaning in to tell him something close to his ear.

They made a striking couple. Ella gorgeously blond and svelte. Eric the proverbial tall, dark and handsome. Not only did they look good together, but they were from the same world.

But they didn't belong together and Eric didn't look at Ella the way he looked at her.

Because he didn't love Ella.

He loved her, Kasey Carmichael.

The thought broke through Kasey's fears. Eric hadn't told her he loved her. Not with words. But he'd shown her. From the night they'd met he'd been showing her how he felt about her. Only she hadn't been paying close enough attention.

Still, she hesitated. What had he thought of Doreen's revelation? Had he given the woman's words any credence?

He loved her. In her heart, she knew he did. Love meant believing in the other person, placing your heart in their hands.

She loved him.

Would trust him with her heart. Even at the risk of having her heart broken.

The music struck up and before she could second-guess herself, Kasey went up to him. "Will you dance with me?"

Ella guffawed.

Eric didn't comment, but he stepped away from Ella and toward the dance floor.

Following him, Kasey bit the inside of her lip. She

wasn't going to run from the way she felt about Eric. Or from her job at Rivendell regardless of what happened.

She wouldn't run. Not ever again.

She'd fight for what she wanted.

What she wanted more than anything was Eric.

That dream was worth fighting for.

Near the middle of the dance floor, he turned to her and Kasey moved into his arms. As always he smelled amazing, felt amazing, was amazing. She wrapped her arms around his neck, toyed with the dark hair brushing his nape and sought the right words.

Thinking wasn't so easy when his powerful body was so close to hers. They moved around the dance floor in perfect accord.

"I'm sorry," she whispered, knowing that was the place to start.

"For?"

"Pushing you away."

"And?"

"I'm going to fight for you, Eric. To my dying breath."

He pulled back to where he could look into her eyes, his gaze narrowed. No light shone in his eyes, no warmth. Had she waited too long? Had he already decided she wasn't worth the effort? Had he believed Doreen Von Buren?

But she owed it to him, and to herself, to lay her heart on the line. "I've kept my heart sheltered because I believed you'd eventually walk away from me and leave me brokenhearted."

"I wasn't the one to walk away," he said, his arms stiff.

"I thought I was beating you to the punch. Up to this

point I haven't trusted you with my heart." She stretched and kissed his cheek. "That's why I'm sorry."

Kasey bit the inside of her lip, watching his face.

The emcee called out Eric's name. Kasey glanced around. The music had stopped, apparently some time ago. Lena, the emcee, Clive Evans and several other suits stood on the stage at the front of the room.

They'd completely missed the song ending, the emcee encouraging people to make donations, and that the emcee had turned the mike over to the clinic's administrator and Clive waited for Eric to join him on the stage.

What had Lena said about their family being honored at the ball?

Eric hesitated, searching her face.

A bit misty-eyed, Kasey pushed against his arm. "Go. I'll tell you everything when you've finished."

Clive read off a list of Eric's accomplishments, both academically and during his work in Africa. Considering what she knew about him, that he'd so completely turned his life around, made her appreciate all the more everything the administrator said.

"It's with great pleasure that I officially welcome Eric to the Rivendell Medical Clinic."

Applause filled the room. Pride filled Kasey. Pride in a man who'd taken control of his life and gave back. To the world. To his community.

To her.

If only she had let him. Please don't let it be too late, she prayed. Please don't let her have pushed Eric away one time too many.

* * *

Eric's mother kissed his cheek, said how proud she was of him, and he was immediately swamped by well-wishers.

What he really wanted was to find Kasey and finish the conversation they'd started. Despite scanning the ballroom, he couldn't spot her anywhere. Had she left? Why was it that each time he got his hopes up that she really cared, that she'd let him behind her shields, she pushed him away?

She'd left her own ball without a lost glass slipper in sight.

"She went out the side door, into the conservatory," his mother whispered into his ear.

"Who?"

She tsked at him. "Don't give me that."

Eric nodded, then paused. He'd promised himself he wasn't going to chase Kasey, that she had to show effort in their relationship, too. Was going into the conservatory after her chasing?

"Go. You know you want to," his mother ordered, pretending to lean in for another kiss to his cheek. "I'll handle this."

She would. There wasn't much his mother couldn't handle.

Eric excused himself and worked his way across the room, eventually sneaking out the conservatory door. It took him a few minutes to find Kasey.

She sat on a bench with a gazebo directly in front of her. Flowers and vines wrapped decoratively around the intricate wrought-iron design. With her gown and tiara, she was straight out of a fairy tale.

She was straight out of his fantasies.

She glanced up, surprise on her lovely face. “Eric. I was expecting you to be tied up for a while. I stepped out to get fresh air.”

Eric sat down on the bench next to her. “We weren’t finished with our conversation.”

“No, we weren’t.” She hesitated, then looked up with eyes so big, so green he felt he could fall into them and never escape. “Doreen Von Buren told me she’d talked to you about visiting Randall.”

“She did.”

“And?”

“And nothing. Doreen is a busybody who stuck her nose where it doesn’t belong.”

Kasey nodded, glanced down at her hands, then back up at him. “Did you believe her?”

“No. Should I have?”

She slipped the glittery mask from her face. Her eyes sparkled as brightly as the costume accessory she’d removed. “This probably isn’t the best time or place, but it’s weighing so heavily on my heart, I have to tell you.”

Had he read her wrong inside? Had he yet again thought Kasey was going to let him in only to discover that she’d changed her mind? “What now?”

“I love you.”

“You love me?”

Kasey stroked her fingers over his jaw, cupped his chin. “More than I ever thought possible. I’m not sure when it happened exactly, maybe I loved you from that very first night, but just refused to see the truth.”

Eric's pulse sped up, slamming through his body. "I love you, too, Kasey, but I'm not sure it's enough."

Kasey's face paled, her fingers trembled against his cheek. "It's enough for me."

"My love?"

She nodded. "For so long I thought I had to have it all. All the things I didn't have growing up. Money, respect, success. I obsessed about having those things. Then I met you and was terrified to love a man who has the world at his fingertips."

"The things that matter can't be bought. Surely you know that by now."

"It took meeting you to figure that one out, but I do know now." At his confused look, she explained. "I blamed everything that went wrong during my childhood on being poor, on being at the bottom of the social food chain. My goals all evolved around making something of myself, having money and social status. I've spent my entire life trying to make up to myself for all the things I never had."

"Wanting a better life isn't a bad thing, Kasey."

"No, except I was chasing after all the things I never had except for the one thing that I'd been missing most. Love."

"What about Randall?"

Kasey took a deep breath. "As much as I'd like to deny it, Doreen was partly right. Randall falls into the successful life category rather than the love. I picked him out as the perfect man to share my life with, spent a year with him thinking that's what would happen. I was too blinded by my goals to see him for the person he really was," she admitted on a sad note. "I'm thankful he didn't think I was good enough for him. If he had, I'd be trapped in a miserable marriage to a man I didn't love and who didn't love me. I'd have missed out on the best thing to happen to me. Falling in love with you. I'm so sorry I pushed you away, Eric."

Eric was an emotional mess and all because of the woman sitting next to him with her big green eyes full of love.

Love. Kasey loved him.

"The only other person to ever push me away was my father," he admitted, knowing he had some explaining of his own to do. "When he realized I would never live up to his expectations, he washed his hands of me. You already know what happened after that. When you refused to let me close, part of me worried I'd never live up to your expectations either. So I didn't fight for you as hard as I should have. I want to live up to your expectations, Kasey. I want to be the man you need in your life. The man to make your world a better place, because you make my world better just by being in it."

Tears streamed down Kasey's cheeks.

He brushed a wet drop away with his fingertip. "Tell me again."

She searched his eyes, caressed his face. "I love you, Eric. With all of my heart, all of my being. I want to spend the rest of my life proving to you how much I love you."

He grinned. "The rest of your life?"

She blushed. "I didn't mean… I…"

"I want the rest of your life, Kasey," he assured her. "I want every breath you take to be mine. Marry me."

Happiness shining in her eyes, Kasey nodded. "Yes."

Knowing love would guide them, Eric leaned down and stole Kasey's breath for all time.

EPILOGUE

WITH shaking hands, Kasey clipped the giant red ribbon adorning the front of RLS's newest pet project, the Betsy Carmichael Health Care for All Center. The clinic was a subsidiary of the Rivendell Medical Center whose sole purpose was to provide health care to the uninsured.

The small crowd cheered as the ribbon ends floated to the concrete walkway.

"I'm so proud of you," Eric whispered close to her ear, their daughter held in his arms.

Erica Carmichael Matthews automatically closed her tiny fists around a lock of her mother's loose hair. Kasey almost always wore her hair down these days. She almost always wore a smile, too.

Just as she was smiling at the moment.

"She's got me again."

"I've got her trained to keep a close hold on you." Eric winked, disengaging their nine-month-old daughter's fingers.

"Here, hand her to me before she musses Kasey's hair," Lena said, reaching for her granddaughter. "There are still press photos to be taken. As the director for this center, Kasey will want to look her best."

"Oh, a little messy hair never hurt anyone," Eric teased, giving Kasey a look that said he'd quite enjoy mussing her hair.

"Of course not." Lena's voice magically transformed as she turned her attention to the apple of her eye, pressing a kiss to the little girl's cherubic cheek. "They think no one noticed Kasey's hair was no longer pinned up after they disappeared from their wedding reception. Photos don't lie."

Kasey and Eric exchanged a look, both smothering laughter. Lena did her best to keep them presentable. Most of the time they complied.

"If you'll all step closer together, we'll get a family shot for the write-up on the clinic's opening."

Eric put his arm around Kasey, pulling her close. Lena stood proudly next to them, holding their precious daughter.

Kasey knew that their road wouldn't always be easy, but when she smiled at the camera with her family around her, her smile was real.

Just as she and Eric's love was real and always would be.

JUNE 2009 LARGE PRINT TITLES

ROMANCE

The Ruthless Magnate's Virgin Mistress	Lynne Graham
The Greek's Forced Bride	Michelle Reid
The Sheikh's Rebellious Mistress	Sandra Marton
The Prince's Waitress Wife	Sarah Morgan
The Australian's Society Bride	Margaret Way
The Royal Marriage Arrangement	Rebecca Winters
Two Little Miracles	Caroline Anderson
Manhattan Boss, Diamond Proposal	Trish Wylie

HISTORICAL

Marrying the Mistress	Juliet Landon
To Deceive a Duke	Amanda McCabe
Knight of Grace	Sophia James

MEDICAL™

A Mummy for Christmas	Caroline Anderson
A Bride and Child Worth Waiting For	Marion Lennox
One Magical Christmas	Carol Marinelli
The GP's Meant-To-Be Bride	Jennifer Taylor
The Italian Surgeon's Christmas Miracle	Alison Roberts
Children's Doctor, Christmas Bride	Lucy Clark

0609 Gen Std HB

MILLS & BOON®

Pure reading pleasure™

JULY 2009 HARDBACK TITLES

ROMANCE

Marchese's Forgotten Bride	Michelle Reid
The Brazilian Millionaire's Love-Child	Anne Mather
Powerful Greek, Unworldly Wife	Sarah Morgan
The Virgin Secretary's Impossible Boss	Carole Mortimer
Kyriakis's Innocent Mistress	Diana Hamilton
Rich, Ruthless and Secretly Royal	Robyn Donald
Spanish Aristocrat, Forced Bride	India Grey
Kept for Her Baby	Kate Walker
The Costanzo Baby Secret	Catherine Spencer
The Mediterranean's Wife by Contract	Kathryn Ross
Claimed: Secret Royal Son	Marion Lennox
Expecting Miracle Twins	Barbara Hannay
A Trip with the Tycoon	Nicola Marsh
Invitation to the Boss's Ball	Fiona Harper
Keeping Her Baby's Secret	Raye Morgan
Memo: The Billionaire's Proposal	Melissa McClone
Secret Sheikh, Secret Baby	Carol Marinelli
The Playboy Doctor's Surprise Proposal	Anne Fraser

HISTORICAL

The Piratical Miss Ravenhurst	Louise Allen
His Forbidden Liaison	Joanna Maitland
An Innocent Debutante in Hanover Square	Anne Herries

MEDICAL™

Pregnant Midwife: Father Needed	Fiona McArthur
His Baby Bombshell	Jessica Matthews
Found: A Mother for His Son	Dianne Drake
Hired: GP and Wife	Judy Campbell

JULY 2009 LARGE PRINT TITLES

ROMANCE

Captive At The Sicilian Billionaire's Command	Penny Jordan
The Greek's Million-Dollar Baby Bargain	Julia James
Bedded for the Spaniard's Pleasure	Carole Mortimer
At the Argentinean Billionaire's Bidding	India Grey
Italian Groom, Princess Bride	Rebecca Winters
Falling for her Convenient Husband	Jessica Steele
Cinderella's Wedding Wish	Jessica Hart
The Rebel Heir's Bride	Patricia Thayer

HISTORICAL

The Rake's Defiant Mistress	Mary Brendan
The Viscount Claims His Bride	Bronwyn Scott
The Major and the Country Miss	Dorothy Elbury

MEDICAL™

The Greek Doctor's New-Year Baby	Kate Hardy
The Heart Surgeon's Secret Child	Meredith Webber
The Midwife's Little Miracle	Fiona McArthur
The Single Dad's New-Year Bride	Amy Andrews
The Wife He's Been Waiting For	Dianne Drake
Posh Doc Claims His Bride	Anne Fraser